THE TRAIN TO PORT ARTHUR

and other stories

THE TRAIN TO PORT ARTHUR

and other stories

L.M. YOUNG

PEONY PRESS
SYLVA, NORTH CAROLINA

Peony Paperback Fiction
Peony Press
Sylva, North Carolina

The stories in this collection are works of fiction. Names, characters, places and incidents either are products of the author's imagination or are used fictitiously. Any resemblance to actual events or locales or persons, living or dead, is entirely coincidental.

"The Cosmetologist" originally appeared in *The Bishop's House Review,* a Duke University publication.

First Printing, 2000

Composed by allpoints, Asheville, North Carolina

Cover design by Celia Naranjo

Cover photo by Ouida Young

Many thanks to Thomas Rain Crowe for his work on the editing of the text and for the production values that went into the making of this book.

Manufactured in the United States of America

10 9 8 7 6 5 4 3 2 1

Library of Congress number:
ISBN 0-9701189-0-2

For ordering information regarding the purchase of this book or other Peony Press publications, e-mail: nita.cowart@gte.net.

CONTENTS

To my Sister

for time, a place and love

I

DEATH AND WITNESSES

A new life! That was what he wanted. That was what he was waiting for. Surely he had begun it already. He had spared one innocent thing, at any rate. He would never again tempt innocence. He would be good.

Oscar Wilde
The Picture of Dorian Gray

PINCH

My best friend Pinch was murdered while I slept. The police reported that she was caught off guard, snuck up on, as Pinch would have said. I don't believe that for one blasted minute. I know she looked her killer in the eye, sized him up, laughed, then spit in his face. It all happened before my very eyes. I had dreamed about her death for the past year.

In May of 1998, the New Orleans Social Services Office finally got divine guidance and mandated that all social workers had to have a partner. This "buddy" would be assigned by the division. The new directive came as a result of what the *Times-Picayune* dubbed The Foster Child Murders. Nine children had been murdered in the last year, "suffocated tenderly," said the Medical Examiner, their bodies placed in the back seat of the city's trolleys. "Fragile spirits fluttering into the moss latticed oaks, riding to God on the St. Charles line." The children had already endured endless and unexplainable pain during their short time among brutal adults. Sexual abuse, torture, starvation, all criminal in their lack of connection with life. One of the trolley drivers, a black man who had worked the Canal Street lines for over forty years and had witnessed life on the mean streets, broke down in front of the cameras and wept. He said he saw a fine mist swirl around the child he had found, a little black girl of six years old. The "dancing fog" vanished into popping fireflies as he approached her. The same Medical Examiner, always there for public events, used the word "reposed," saying that in all his years working on the most vicious murders, this was the first time he was truly terrified. "When I cut them open," he told a reporter, "I saw their little souls rise up, and then I heard a child giggle." His name was Harlen Boudreaux and he retired after autopsying the ninth child.

My name is Hannah DuBois. I am a social worker assigned to investigate child abuse cases in the most forgotten areas of the heavenly city of New Orleans. After my first two years on the job, I stopped seeing the perpetrators as pathological. They were simply evil, doomed, without hope of redemption. Evil is evil no matter how many times you toss the coin. I had met five of the murdered foster children during some initial investigations; two were my cases and I had placed them in foster care.

Tasha and Kenneth were lucky I thought; they had gone to caring foster parents. Tasha was the ninth child, and it was a week after her death that I was partnered.

Earlene Washington became my buddy. She had already been my friend for five years. We had shared our failures as potential social saviors, but had never allowed each other to give up. Earlene had grown up in the New Orleans Projects, had tried just about every street drug by the time she was twelve. She stole to keep from going hungry, acquiring the nickname Pinch. I grew up on a farm between New Orleans and Baton Rouge. My grandparents did not speak English and my mother stopped talking altogether the night my father went to town for a beer and never came back. I dreamed day and night, had visions that caused my banishment from our parish Catholic Church. Only saints have visions, I suppose. I grew up poor, was sixteen before I ate pizza, and saved almost every dime I made. My pockets were stuffed with crackers, and sugar, mustard and ketchup packets from fast food joints. "Want not" was my motto. So Pinch nicknamed me Scrimp. We made quite a pair.

They say that cops routinely dream about their partners' death. So why should it be different for social workers? The day after Pinch became my buddy, I started to see her murder, clear as I see myself in my bathroom mirror, in the soap and grease encrusted mirror at work and in the mirror that is Pinch's eyes. I told her about it, about how sometimes what I saw in my mind came true, how other times I just couldn't know because it happened in places far away. She said she understood. Her grandmother practiced voodoo. I didn't tell her that her murderer is a ghost, a haunting, a fiend, evil.

I had to identify her body. Her eyes had been gouged out, her cheeks slashed with a sharp knife or maybe a razor blade. The devil had run her through with an ancient pirate's sword that was later traced to the Cabildo. It had been stolen from that museum a week before Mardi Gras. Beautiful, desecrated Pinch.

Pinch was buried next to her mother in a graveyard that had endured since the Civil War. Out of deference to history and remembrance, the community had left a wooden sign that read: *Colored Cemetery*. It rained straight down on me as I stood watching her casket descend into the ground. Ninety-five degrees and raining, I heard someone whisper. Steam rose off the bodies standing around Pinch's grave. She came to me that night, as my head lolled on my arms, the vodka haze barely masking my memory of her. She caressed my head and told me not to worry. *Come on Scrimp. Girl, you know I'd never leave my buddy.*

I woke up to the dull New Orleans sun streaking onto my bed and the memory of Pinch comforting me. She had been a heartbeat away.

"Well, partner, it's about time you rise and shine."

"Stop it!" I yelled, slapping my hands over my face.

"Scrimp. You'll have to face it. It's me, Pinch. No dream, no voodoo. Just little ol' bad ass me."

A moment can be an eternity. "Pinch?" I said as I let my hands fall to the bed and looked at the tattered wicker rocking chair next to the window. It rocked in time with the tapping of the palm fronds on the windowpane. A rainbow of color formed the outline of a body that moved upward and towards me, hands outstretched, arms waving, and then slipping down beside me on the bed. A cool and joyful mist entered me. I turned toward the head, seeing eyes that had yellow points, like popping fireflies. Now Pinch was golden brown, her once chocolate skin sparkling. I smelled sweet fudge. Her wide, thick mouth was her clearest feature. She smiled at me.

"So, Scrimp, what do you think? Pretty nifty, huh? Don't be afraid. Lay down, sleep with me, get used to this."

And I did.

"How long can you stay here, Pinch, on earth?" I was on my third cup of strong coffee and chicory, made thick with white cream and sweet with lots of raw cane sugar.

"As long as I'm busy, I can stay."

"What do you mean?" I asked, hoping she meant a long time.

"Doing something, I got to be doing something. Not just sitting around spying on everybody. So far only you can see me."

"Pinch, I saw you die. In my dreams. A ghost killed you, didn't he? It."

"Oh, *it* was a *he* alright. At least a former he."

"So how come he can be here if ghosts got to do something?"

"Nobody says it has to be a good something," she laughed, then tinkled, like put-back-together glass dancing through the room. "Good old Scrimp. Still thinks the world can be good."

"Yes, but the key word is capacity."

"Fine."

"So if you do something, you can stay with me a long time?"

"Yes. And as time moves on, the clearer I'll get to you."

I walked out to the balcony of my apartment. I lived in the French Quarters, about three blocks from Royal Street. Midday smells infused the Saturday air. Mrs. Mendoza was cooking sweet *andouille* sausage and onions. In the courtyard two of my neighbor's children sped around the bubbling fountain on big wheels. The trickling water grew louder, like an avalanche, then again the mutated shattering glass played with the air. A blue mist rose up beyond the rooftops and scurried away like banished haunts, towards the Mississippi. A steamboat tooted a lonesome sound that shook me to the core.

"Time is endless, Scrimp," said Pinch.

I turned toward her and smiled. "Can we still be partners?"

"Sho nuf," she tinkled. "Them honky cops of yours and the big bad brothers of mine cain't find their own dicks in the dark, seems like."

"Now you're sounding more like Pinch," I laughed, reaching out to her, my left hand slowly moving to her shoulder and then dissolving into her body. Again fireflies danced. "Will it do that every time I touch you?"

"Yes. But I think you'll start to feel something one day. Substantial me."

"I think I already do."

"I'll be near you just about all the time. I can get into places you can't. Eavesdrop. What a team we'll make. But I can't fight for you. My body'll just go through them. I'm the thinker now."

"Don't let it go to your head."

I took a four-week leave from work. My supervisor knew that Pinch and I had been close. Pinch went with me to the library, poured through police reports on the Foster Child Murders, and inspected the trolleys while I talked to the drivers for what must have been their twentieth interview. They were all good people. The night before I was to go back to work, I decided to try my idea out on Pinch.

"I go back to work tomorrow. They'll give me another partner. I don't want that," I said."Then what's on your mind, Scrimp? Out with it."

"We need to find out who killed the kids. Find the ghost. Maybe it's the same one that killed you. The police have zilch. Good God, I see another murder soon, Pinch!"

Her words came to me slowly, like she had gone underwater. "Go on. What's the whole plan?"

"I want to start my own business. Investigations. So we don't have to follow those shitty bureaucratic rules anymore. We both hated the system, didn't we Pinch?"

"Yes. But, at the time it was all we had to work with."

"Right! You see, you're right there with me. Oh wow!"

"Don't you need a license?"

"No. I've thought about that. It will be a consulting company. Social consulting. Come on, this is America. You can start a business doing anything. I have a degree in social work. I checked the law, and I can do it."

"Well, it sounds like my death gave you your opportunity," she said.

"Oh, Pinch, I didn't mean it to come out that way. I'm sorry."

"I'm kidding you, friend. I'm all for it. What a time we will have!"

"I'll call it: Pinch and Scrimp Consulting."

"Ah, how will you explain my name? I'm dead, remember?"

"Oh, that's easy. I'll just say how I admired you, loved you because you were my best friend, that you were the greatest partner that ever lived. It'll be one of those *in memory of* things."

"Don't lay the mushy stuff about me on too thick, okay. I had to die to finally get a piece of the American dream. Would you say I was a ghost of an entrepreneur?"

I walked over to the window. The sun was moving below the rooftops. I puffed my breath onto the glass making steam and wrote the letters P and S with my finger. I felt Pinch next to me, saw another puff of steam on the window, then sparkling mist and tinkling laughter. "Hello friend," I said.

The tenth child was found on the trolley that made its last stop in front of the now deserted Stein Department Store. Stein had folded, and armies of trolley riding old women had loss jobs they had worked at since the war. The child was named Theresa Guidry. She was five years old and a foster child since the age of two months. Her body reposed on the back seat, wrapped in a powder blue blanket. Sesame Street characters danced on her tiny yellow sneakers. In her hand she held a small pearl rosary.

THE LADIES ROOM

I had already left civilization, passing through a decent sized central Florida town. I had tanked the car and bought a value meal at Burger King. Now the smell of oil suddenly mixed with the hamburger and the anxiety of the open road. My stomach turned as I looked to each side of the road for a place to stop. The book tape readings still droned from the back speakers. A lilting English accent described the Vampire Pandora's heightened sense of Antioch. This was definitely adding to my now surreal predicament. Anne Rice would appreciate this. Bleak setting. Vampires getting me ready for the corrupt city nights of Florida. I reached out and turned off the tape, canceling my pleasant journey to the coast. Instead, I sputtered, clanked and absorbed the foul air of my own miserable mistake.

I glimpsed at a few old shacks passing by, as though I were the one motionless. No gas stations, no convenience stores beckoned to me. I pushed down on the accelerator again, hoping that I would find a place soon, willing my heart to slow down. I repeated my anti-panic mantra, *ohm, ohm* and then whispered, "Jesus, help me."

There it was, appearing out of the Florida scrub. A low hanging, dark brown building. Trucks were lined up in front of double glass doors. I looked for a sign, something to tell me that here I would get help. I looked to the roof of the building, tin reflected the shining, hot sun, with a black pole rising into the air. A dark shadow was silhouetted against a large, white puffy cloud. My eyes adjusted to the glare and I beheld a great and shining neon green alligator. Flashing blue letters rode on top of the alligator's back, announcing to all who passed here that this was the *Watering Hole on 17.*

The *WH* is a place of legend in Central Florida, a place, they say, where no woman should go to alone, ever, and no man alone after nine at night. I aimed my car for the parking spot next to a maroon truck and clanked to a stop. I looked up into the truck's cab; it was empty except for the swaying shadows of the palm trees that dominated the left edge of the building. Dried mud encased the windshield like dark circles under a dying man's eyes. I walked to the front of the truck and toward the entrance to the building, glancing at the Texas license plate. My little sister used to call it the "lonely star state." My last thought before I walked into the *Watering Hole on 17* was that ever since I'd moved to Central Florida five years ago from New York, I had been convinced that werewolves roamed the Florida scrub. Vampires, I knew, were not the stuff of legends. I looked into the face of the searing sun, trying to remember if the earth had entered the cycle of the full moon.

Darkness hit me, and twanging music, and cigarette smoke. I felt the hot air that had followed me in the building escape back outside as the doors swished shut behind me. I blinked, waiting for my eyes to adjust to the dimness. I peered into a dark, dank, hollow cavern; a lair, a hiding place for the yellow piercing eyes of . . .

"Hello there, darlin', can I do you for something? Too early in the afternoon for a little one like you to drink," barked the deep man voice from behind me.

I spun around to meet him, when the heel of my navy blue pump twisted and I fell forward. Arms grabbed me, laughter bounced through my head, and the smell of stale alcohol and vanilla pushed into my stomach. I screamed and pushed the man away, careening backward, my left foot now shoeless.

"What the hell are you trying to do?" I yelled.

"Just trying to help. Heard you pull up. Figured you were in a might of trouble. Sorry. I guess I'll just go back to my wonderings 'stead of acting like a fool gentleman," he mumbled, turning away from me. My eyes adjusted to the darkness as he slid away towards a long bar that was crowned by more blinking neon lights. These announced the types of liquor available. *17 Different Brews*. I looked at a clock that pulsated green and pink. Miniature alligators twirled around time. It was almost one-forty. I picked up my shoe. The heel was gone. I hobbled towards the bar and a large man that, I prayed dear Lord, would just give me the phone so I could call triple A. The floor under my foot was wet and fuzzy. I pushed my hair behind my right ear and wiped my face with my hands. I swear I smelled like the place already, like smoke and lost hope.

"Excuse me, sir. Sir? Hello! Sir!" I didn't want to yell. The last thing I needed was more little darlins and John Wayne attitudes. Next thing I know Charlten Heston'll come slithering through the door. Worst yet, Lon Chaney.

The big, brown back turned slowly. I moved forward and looked up into unexpected kind eyes painted on a face that could scare the bejesus out of Hannibal Lecter. Spreading forehead haloed by a bushy, black head, eyebrows to match, leathered skin, and a wide mouth that smiled, opening to a few brown teeth, black spaces like a jack-o'-lantern.

"Well, how do ya. Are in trouble?" He asked, his voice soft and warm and comforting.

"Yes," I said, "Please, do you have a phone I could use? I need to call triple A. My car is broken down."

"I cain't let you use the bar phone. You have to go to the pay."

"But it's an eight hundred number. It won't cost you anything."

"Sorry, hon. Cain't do. Over there," he said, pointing to the left of the bar.

I followed his finger with my eyes. A doorway with a bright light shining through was about twenty feet away from me. Beyond a row of tables, to the left of the tables, was a small stage. Band instruments and a microphone waited for life to begin in here again. I looked back at the doorway. I could make out a sign above the door. *Ladies.* I looked back at the man, my heart thumping.

"Do you have change for a dollar?" I asked.

As soon as I walked through the doorway, I felt my bladder fill. So much for the power of suggestion versus mind over matter.

There was only one stall in the mustard yellowed ladies room. The mirror over the sink was soiled; rivers of embroidered soap and red lipstick covered most of the glass. Red words made me jerk my head backward, pinching the nerve at the base of my skull. Oblongata, I thought suddenly, then I whispered the words to my own distorted reflection: *Help me, you dog.*

An urge can be overwhelming; nerves travel down within less than nanoseconds. I pushed on the door of the stall, but nothing happened. I took in air and the acid fumes of old urine and pine made me gag. I bent over, twisting my head and stared at a pair of brown cowboy boots enveloped by crumpled dark blue jeans.

"I'm sorry, " I said, "but will you be long?"

Nothing. Silence, but for the buzzing and clicking of the ceiling light. The legs did not move.

"Hello. Are you alright?" I asked. "Lady, come on. Are you alright?"

Squinting my left eye, I looked through the crack between the door and the metal casing. Blond hair covered a head that was bent forward. The person had a white shirt on, and I could detect no movement of the chest. I counted to ten, then pushed hard on the door. It whined open and hit the body. The woman's head popped back, her blue eyes were like cats eye marbles that were sizing up the cosmos.

Her face was chalk white. Ribbons of her hair lay pasted over the sides of her face. Cobalt lips protruded like a blowfish. Lady's arms draped scarecrow-like at her sides. I knew she was dead, yet I was not afraid and the urge to pee left me. I felt a sense of control take hold of me. I bent over to look at her closely: young, maybe twenty, pretty in life, desolate in death, a thin waif whose life had ended in this place where no woman should come to alone. But she did, maybe stranded like me, afraid, more trusting. And I smelled vanilla, as I traced the purple bruise from one side of her neck to the other with my finger, careful not to actually touch her.

I backed out of the stall while reaching into my jacket pocket for the change the big man behind the bar had given me. I unfolded a Kleenex at the bottom of my pocket and excised an old chewed piece of gum that had hardened. It was probably over a year old. With the Kleenex draped over the knob, I carefully pulled on the wooden door, like I'd read in detective novels. Raymond and Archie and Kaye and Kinsey be with me I chanted.

The public telephone was to my right. A chain dangled to the floor, having once possessed the telephone book for a brief moment. Who, I wondered, stole telephone books? I lifted the dirty receiver, tipping the mouthpiece as far away from my mouth as possible, deposited fifty cents and pressed 911 just as I heard the loud flush of a toilet to my left. I glanced in the direction of the sound and to a moss green, scaly door of the "Man's Room."

"Nine-one-one, can I help you?"

"Help, yes, help. I found a body. Dead. On the toilet!"

"Ah, on the toilet? Where are you, ma'am?"

"U.S. seventeen. A place called the Watering . . ."

The hand came down on the phone like a sledgehammer and I felt myself crushed against the wall. The world darkened and I smelled the scent of my mother's baking. She had always used vanilla extract.

"Are you all right? Ma'am, can you get up?" Said the voice that I recognized, as my mind adjusted to consciousness. Big man from behind the bar stood over me, his brows drawn together in concern, his eyes wide in questioning.

"A man pushed me. And there's a dead lady in the restroom," I groaned, wiping away spit from the corner of my mouth. I felt hands lift me and position me against the wall.

"The police are coming. They already got a call from here. Somebody told them they's a body here. I called, too, when I found you. I got worried when you didn't come out."

"That was me. I guess the operator knows this place," I said, "and thanks for worrying about me."

"Okay."

"Did you see a man run out? I think it was the same one I saw when I came in. I bumped into him."

"No, he maybe went out the back."

"And the dead lady?"

"I don't know any lady. I just came to work a little before you got here."

"I see," I said, studying him, hoping that he was telling me the truth. I had a lot to tell the police.

The state police are a fast organization, I can attest to that. They arrived in about five minutes and found me sampling beer number seventeen on the list of solutions to life's problems. It was brewed in China, a long way away from here. And I told all I suspected as the nice policeman listened to me patiently. Dead lady was driving the truck that's still parked next to mine. Dried mud shows that it's been there a long time. No rain has come to this land for days now to wash the mud away. There is no mud like that around Florida, is there? The man I ran into I know is the same one that banged me into the wall. I smelled vanilla on him and on the lady. Yes, I can describe him, I guarantee. I will be available if I'm needed to ID him. Poor lady, coming here in distress, she probably had no choice late at night. I bet there was no phone in her car and she was looking for a pay phone and a drink. Was she running, I asked him. Probably, he said. Women should take better precautions when traveling alone. The big man behind the bar said he never saw her come in. He doesn't come into work until the afternoon.

"You haven't said hi to Mike," said big man. "Everyone who comes here says hi to Mike."

"Mike?" I asked.

"Yeah, our alligator. He's special."

"Special? Okay," I said, turning to the nice policeman. "I'm going to meet Mike."

"Sure thing," he said, nodding and continuing to write on his clipboard. I guessed he had already met Mike.

I followed big man down the hall that led to the Ladies Room. The passage to the left was tapped off, just like in the movies. We turned left down an unlit passage. I heard a loud click and felt the blast of bright, hot sunlight.

"This way," I heard him laugh.

We were outside. Before me was a large pond. Pine trees lined it on the left, and on the right a forlorn Jacaranda tree trembled. Its lavender blossoms had already followed the winds away from here, leaving the curled kidney shaped black pods clacking like the swift hands of a flamingo dancer. A barbed wire fence, about six feet high, formed a total enclosure around the pond.

"Where's Mike?" I asked.

"Over on the other side. You see his head sticking out? Looks like a log with two big knobs."

"Yes. Hi Mike, nice meetin' ya," I whispered, turning to big man, searching his face, his green eyes giving off yellow sparks. "Is Mike a tourist attraction?"

"Oh, no ma'am. He's ours. A local mascot, you'd call him. Mike is one of us. Keeps things cleaned up around here. Gators eat trash," he said, laughter in his voice.

"How long has he been here in this pond?" I asked, holding tears back, watching Mike as he slowly glided towards me.

"Seems like forever, " he said.

REVENGE

I was thirteen when my mother taught me how to shoot a gun. I can still smell the metallic grease, feel the .38 fit snugly in my hand, and see the black silhouette of the target. Mom's hand covered mine, her left thumb shifting my trigger finger into a better position. Pointed red fingernails flashed in the sun. Perspiration burned like tears. It was so damn hot. Her throaty smoker's voice cooed to me: "Now, Amy, look at the man target with your right eye. See his heart? Think about it thumping. Start counting until you can hear the thumps. Feel them, then count to ten thumps, hold steady, and pull the trigger."

Nine lonely years have gone by. Mom was not only murdered, but raped, her cold body dumped in an empty lot off of Eucalyptus Avenue. It happened one year almost to the day after I had completed those target lessons. I will never forget any details of the day she died. It was my birthday. July 6 and south Florida now have only two meanings for me: heat and revenge. They found her body three weeks after Daddy reported her missing. So, in the heat, well, what's a daughter to say? It's enough I dream about her; it's the only way I know what she looked like. And today is happy revenge day.

My strategy has been formulated over the years. I've taken measured steps, written events and dates down on legal paper and put them in a safe deposit box day by day, week by week, month by month, year by year, with all the other documents I've stolen and copied. I have pictures, too. Pictures of ruin I call them. I could blackmail the whole crappy town council of Cornersville, if I wanted to. But I won't. I used to have only suspicions. But, last May I found the proof. Yes, I know exactly who killed my mother. And he's going to pay big time.

Breyer's Contracting Services is located at the end of Main Street. Palm trees and red topped oleanders line the road leading to the business offices, their heads swaying in the summer breeze, brushing the barbed wire on the towering chain link fence. When I drive to work in the mornings, it's like riding to my death, like maybe Jesus felt in Gethsemane. Cold, lonely and betrayed. Dauchau-like. The air is bloated with the acid stench of burning rubber. My usual parking place is to the right of the large glass doors that announce **ENTRANCE** in big, black letters. A purple Glory bush once greeted me, but died when the boss's son J.D. Breyer, Jr., or J.D. as he's called, poured old engine oil on it. "The environment be damned," he said when I complained. So be it. I expect this to be my last funeral ride.

"Hey, Amy," yells Sparky Smythe, "Ya cain't park hea." He is the chief contractor and a complete ass hole. He leans into my car window; his fat, red freckled nose is almost touching my cheek. I can't look at him. I know that his eyes are glazed, rummy, and that sweat is oozing from his pocked pores like an affliction, pooling in the river-like scars that gash across his right cheek. It is enough that I smell alcohol mixed with his body odor. I swallow several times, keeping my skimpy breakfast of toast and coffee down. I am glad I couldn't eat much more this morning.

"What's wrong with parking here? I always park here," I say, without emotion, my eyes straight ahead. No contact, I think, as I hold my breath.

"I needs it fa da dump trucks. We cleaning the place out," he breathes the foul words on my face.

I turn on him, confused, fear running through me like the streams from an erupted volcano, like you see on the Discovery Channel. The last papers that will complete my plans are in there. My head screeches. It was supposed to be a day like every day here. Normal, not cleaning the place out. Spit bubbles from the sides of Sparky's grimacing mouth. It is froth from a bad dog.

"Cleaning the place out?" I ask. "What the hell are you talking about?"

"Doan ask me, darlin'. Ask J.D."

My name is Amy McDoogal and I am the Administrative Secretary to J.D. Breyer, Senior. It says so on the nameplate in the middle of my mahogany desk. The one that was ripped from the Rain Forest. Surprisingly, I dated J.D., Junior on and off for the last four years, until he tried to get me into bed against my better taste. So, I broke it off for good. I had gotten as much information that I could from him. But J.D. Senior is behind it all. The last shreds of paper that I need to send them all to hell is in his office. I have to get there before the moving crew takes everything away.

Not one item on my desk had been touched. I know because I had made pencil dots next to each thing so that I could tell if anyone had been fooling around; if they suspected me. I tape the drawers shut every evening before I go home. Invisible tape, detecting tools really, can be found with little effort. Kind of like carrying a gun around in your purse, concealed and ready. But it is the chair that alarms me. I always push it in, the tips of the arms just touching the edge of the desk. It is pulled away, just enough to tell me that someone has been sitting at my desk. My computer screen is turned toward the chair, as though someone had used my computer. A wave of tension seizes me, even though I know that there is nothing in the computer files that would point to my investigation, my deception. My mind tries to force an image of who has been here, but nothing comes but fear. In four years, this has never happened. I pull my chair out all the way and check the upholstery. It is clean. What did I expect, blood on the seat?

Senior's office door is closed. He comes to work at nine on the dot. It is only eight fifteen. I believe I am alone in the building at this time of the morning, as usual. If my calculations are right, the FBI will receive the special delivery package I sent yesterday by twelve today. Then I will make my telephone call verifying the information in the package, then another confirmation by fax. This all has to been done by 12:30, but not from the offices of Breyer Contracting Services. My ace is in Senior's office. I need to move fast. The air conditioning system begins humming as it switches on in the utility closet down the hall. I hear no voices. I close my eyes and listen for noises in the building. All is silence, except for the murmuring through the ducts in the ceiling. I take in the good air and let out the bad, counting until I reach twenty, then I will make my move.

"Yo! Amsie, what goes down girlfriend?"

My hands grasp the edge of my desk, and I look up into the face of Mauveen Jackson, the data analyst for the consulting firm that has just completed an audit of our books. Mauveen has led me to many places in the playground of Breyer's accounts. She just doesn't know it. I've felt bad at times, taking advantage of her. But, administrative assistants can get anything they want. Other people don't know that their bosses don't tell them much at all. Senior once told me I had a fine ass. Double damn to you, Senior, nothing like making my will stronger.

"Mo, you scared the crap out of me. Where'd you come from, anyway?" I ask, making light of her intrusion into my space.

"Little girl's room. Been here since seven. Cleaning out and clearing out. Job's finished. Hey, want to have lunch, since it's my last day?"

"Oh, Mo, darn. If I'd known. Sparky's saying the whole place is clearing out. I go home one day and the next the whole place almost disappears on me. Do you know what's going on?"

"Hey, I'm not putting myself on the line. I just count the numbers, babe."

"Come on, Mo, tell. I can help the company if I know. Is it under the table stuff?"

"Okay, just a hint. I'm never coming back to this place, anyway. Man, *how do you stand it?* It's cold in here. I mean people cold. It's back to the big city for me."

"You moving back north?" I ask, trying to change the subject, planning to ask my question at just the right moment. I really hate to do this to Mauveen. She's a nice person.

"No. Tampa. Back to where somethin's happening. This is dull, man. You too young to be wasted here. What gives, anyway? Why you stay here?"

"You know my Daddy works here. He needs me, especially since Mom died.

"Yeh, but that was years ago. She sure don't want you here, I bet. She's looking down from heaven and wishing you in a better place."

"I guess. But, Mo, what did ya'll find? It'll help my job if you tell me."

"I can't see that it will, but okay," she whispers, then leans her elbows on my desk, her face not an inch from mine, and looks into my eyes. "Just a hint. Politics and kickbacks."

"Where's the books?" I ask, my voice a hoarse hissing.

"Can't give you that, hon. All turned over to Junior. We're out of here. Take care, Amy, you've got a lot to lose here. My advice is get out and get a life." I feel myself being pulled into her arms, squeezed, and then she is gone. Like air being let out of a balloon. Good-bye, friend.

I had always kept the key to Senior's office on a long chain around my neck. I had made the impression of the key one night when J.D. had gone to the bathroom at my apartment. He had left his suit jacket on the chair and luck had given me the chance to make my dreams come true. I watch through the glass doors as Mauveen gets into her canary yellow Mustang and drives away. I check the hallway. Empty. I pull the key from between my breasts, unlock Senior's office door and slide in, pressing my back against the closing door. Gently, gently, I tell myself, and breathe. I am hit by an odor that sends my head spinning. I feel the cold hand of anxiety grip my neck, but I am still standing. It must be less than fifty degrees in here, and I smell the puke of his after-shave, like marshmallows and hay and manure. I imagine cow shit on his boots. I lock the door and put on the lights. There are no windows in this office, so I cannot be detected from the outside. The glare snaps at my eyes until I blink and stare at where Senior's desk used to be. The indentations of the desk's feet still seem to press into the deep gray carpet. My eyes move to the walls. The pink flamingoes that once stood in the crowd of cattails have flown away leaving a bright rectangle on dull white walls. Everything is gone. The cigar smoking face of Senior flashes in my head, and I start to cry. "Oh, Mom," I squeak into my hands, "didn't I do this fast enough? Did I wait too long for revenge?"

I hear voices and banging against the outer wall. My left hand seems to be on automatic as I grab the key and drop it into the front of my blouse. The chain feels like a snake against my skin. My ear is pressed to the door and the sounds ebb down the hall. I leave Senior's now caverned office and head for the ladies room. I must think, retrench, continue on my mission.

"The picture can be discerned with one piece of the puzzle missing," I say to the mirror as I lift my face from the cool splash of water from the sink. I read that in some detective novel. I can't remember which one. I'm confused, but I will not panic. My eyes are red, the rose lipstick gone, my long blond hair is held in place by a blue headband. You look like Tipper Gore, J.D. had told me one day. *Innocent.* The natural porcelain of my skin contrasts the black eyes that stare at me. I look like a doll whose maker forgot to paint color into its being. I wonder if I still know who I am. This is what it must feel like to be an alcoholic. I suppress the rising anxiety and step towards the door. I will wait at my desk until it is time to contact the FBI.

J.D. is waiting for me. He is sitting on the corner of my desk, one leg draping down, a winged tip oxford touching the floor.

"Well, Amy, I suppose you've figured out what's going on?"

"No, I really haven't. I wasn't told about any of this. Whatever *this* is. Want to tell me?"

"Just think, sweetheart, Daddy Senior's been arrested. Fraud, kickbacks and, believe it or not, a little payoff at the polls for the last ten years of elections. Hot shit, huh? I wonder who turned him in?"

I can't speak. I try to swallow, but a fist is pushing down my throat. My eyes are burning because I'm trying not to cry, not to fly into little pieces and scatter all over the universe. My God, I think, how did they find out it was me so fast? I thought the FBI would keep it secret.

"You look all shook up. Please. You hated him as much as I did. I had to do it," he says. His crystal green cat eyes are sparkling, the mouth laughing like it's no longer part of his face, his sun-streaked brown hair waves to the left of his head. His tie is knotted so tight I wait for his Adam's apple to burst. I used to think he was so handsome. I even liked him a little. Now he is the devil. He has ruined it all.

"You turned in your own father?" I am hissing like a sick raccoon. "But, why? You have everything you want. Please don't tell me it's because you believe in justice or doing the right thing. I know you better than that."

"You're right. I just want it all. But I want it fair and square. You know, I never understood why people make their lives so complicated by getting into illegal stuff. Do you understand it, Amy?" he asks, pulling at the tips of my hair, then rubbing the small of my back.

"Maybe they think they'll never get caught," I say, stepping backward and away from him.

"The odds are against it. Well, hold on to your hat, little one, there's more arrests coming down. Dad was not a careful man. He's pulling a whole lot of people down with him."

"Who?" I ask.

"Amy, look, I like you. I always have. You're a good person and I know what your life has been like here. I never figured why you stayed. You're beautiful and smart, whether you want anyone to know or not. But, your father. . .."

"No! No, goddammit, you're not going to take him away from me, too! He didn't have anything to do with this! He's just an accountant. Don't take him away! No!" I hear myself scream as I rush at J.D., beating at him with my fists.

"Stop it! Hell, Amy, stop it," he grunts, pushing me away. "He's been part of it for years. Even when we were kids it was going on. Up to the top of his head."

"No. You're a dirty, rat liar, just like your father! A stinking liar. I'll kill all of you!" I shout as I run out of the building.

Fear. I know what fear is. I live with anxiety attacks and it's like living on the edge of the world, just waiting to fall off. It begins with the air closing in, then the tingling of my toes and fingertips. I wait for the hot hands to massage my face. Heat seeps from the electrified membranes of my skin and I smell the uncontrolled release of fluids from all the openings of my body, like old men who don't bathe. Sour death. The hand rises from my stomach and squeezes my chest. The thumping of my heart is a pump in my ears, just like the man target heart I want to stop. It goes faster, faster until I want to shriek *Dear Lord in heaven, help me!*

There are only three Xanax tablets left in the bottle. I carefully line them up on the table, neon white against the sun yellow Formica. One, two, three, then a half of a glass of water. I look at the digital clock on the kitchen counter, red letters flipping time. It is three o'clock in the afternoon. "One now," I say to myself, "then another in an hour, then another one more hour later." I pick up one pill with my left hand, hold it in front of me, and then ease it onto my tongue, like the steel cranes at Breyer's Contracting Service. I push my head back and pour water into my upturned mouth. I taste the bitter pill for just an instant. I'll wait for relief and then I'll get the .38 and visit Daddy in the city jail.

Barry Banfield was elected Sheriff of Cornnersville five times in a row for two-year terms. He has been sheriff for ten years. Matter of fact, he was running for reelection the year Mom died. He used to come to our house for supper on Saturday nights. Mom really liked him. I could tell. She said he was funny, and once slipped when we were doing the dishes and said he was sexy. He waits for me now; his feet propped up on his desk, toothpick sliding back and forth in his mouth. I can't see what Mom saw in him. Do the years change a person that much? He is fat. His body is stuffed into his shirt, his stomach rising like a giant helium balloon as he leans backward. He is wearing a white cowboy hat that is stained with his oily sweat.

"Amy, darlin', come on in. Sit. Sorry about ya Dad, but I had to arrest him, ya know it."

"Don't call me *darlin*. There's blood on your hands," I say, staring at him, standing in front of his desk, almost touching his boots with my stomach.

"Look it girl, I know your upset, but it's no time for accusing. You're talking crazy."

"Am I? I want to see my father. Now."

"He's being booked. You'd better understand that he's committed federal crimes. The FBI is here. I cain't control a damn thing that's going on," he says. He stands up and walks towards me, not stopping until he is almost touching me with his body. I look up and see the hair in his nose.

I squint at him and bite my lips. "Who can I talk to, then?"

"Listen, I'll ask if they can make you a special case. Girl oughta be able to see her Daddy. Use my office. Wait here, sweetheart."

My father's eyes are like deep, black pools. His eyebrows are long and fall forward over his eyes like hanging moss. They are completely gray, like the hair on his head and arms. When I was little, I thought he looked like a lion. To me he was strong, with arms that wrapped me in a soft, dark shell when we played the turtle game. I was safe inside that shell. He sits before me now forever changed. He has grown thin over the years, his skin blending with his hair as though he will disappear any minute. Now I see it is camouflage. The lion has turned into a hyena.

"Well, Daddy. Did you do what they said?" I ask, my hands folded in my lap, my emerald green skirt pulled over my knees, complementing the redness of my fingernails. I think of Christmas. "You have to tell me the truth, otherwise I will have nothing left."

"No, honey, Please. You have your whole life before you. Get out of this town. Forget about me. *Please*." He reaches for my hands, staring into my eyes, black eyes to black eyes, but I pull away from him and wrap my arms around my body. "I went along with Senior because of you. To protect you, give you a decent life."

"What? A decent life? Stuck in this hellhole of a town. Every day reminded of my mother. I smell her rotting flesh in this town. I've spent all these years waiting to get even with Senior. Now you've ruined it. You betrayed me!"

"I don't know what you're talking about," he mumbles. He stands. I see tears in his eyes. "*Amy, what are you talking about?*" It is in his face. He understands .

"I want revenge. You took it from me," I say, standing. I slip my hand in my purse and feel the cold metal.

"Your mother was a whore. She slept with every man at Breyer's. Even on Christmas night I found her with him. I had to protect you from knowing that. That's why I went along with Senior's payoffs."

"You fixed the books for him?"

"Yes."

"You did it because you're a wimp. You were scared of Senior. We could have just left here. Gone to another town, another state. We don't even have family here. Nobody. I'm sorry Daddy. Senior was blackmailing you, wasn't he?"

He gets up from his chair, walks toward me, arms outstretched. "Come on little turtle, come into your shell," comes his soothing voice.

I think about the thumping and close my eyes. *Come on little turtle; come into your shell.* I hear one thump, two thumps then count to ten. I pull the gun from my purse, close my right eye and see the black image. I hold steady and pull the trigger.

The hot wind is blowing sand around my father's coffin. Baby sand tornadoes dance around and fall into the crevices around the hole in which he will rest. Mom's grave is next to his. They will rest together. The pastor from the First Baptist Church drones on about love and sacrifice and being a father. I close my eyes tightly and look at the kaleidoscope twirl in the darkness of my lids.

I lose myself in space and time until it is all over. Mourners pay respect, but there is none here today. I open my eyes and see ghosts of people I once worked with, ate with, and shared secrets of my teenage life with. They are transparent now. I smell alcohol and sweat and look into the glazed, filmy eyes of Sparky. He takes my hand as though he was inspecting it for cancer and leans into me, his rancid voice in my ear.

"Red finger nails just like ya Mom, darlin'. A wildcat scratching my face up."

I am falling, a hand has squeezed the life from my heart and the world vanishes.

I am awake. There is only one window in this room. It is not large enough for a child to crawl through even if the bars were removed. But it is low enough so I can see the trees and flowers. A blooming purple Glory bush waves to me. I know I am in a hospital for the mentally ill about ten miles from Cornersville. Our school bus used to pass on the road in front of here when we went to high school band competitions. It was a TB sanitarium, so we held our noses so we wouldn't get sick and die. I played the flute. The walls are a dull off white. There are small holes near the locked door where the previous tenants tried to bang their way out. Sometimes I see eyes looking through the peephole. But I ignore them. I am allowed to tape pictures on the walls. I get them from the old magazines in the sitting room, when I'm let out. I have two pictures. One is of a boat sailing off the coast of the Bahamas. The boat is gently rocking in the sea green water. The sun is shining, but it is not hot. I like the woman's red bathing suit. The other picture shows baby sea turtles under a spotlight. The caption says that they are hurrying to the sea before seagulls eat them. I have one chair, a desk with no drawers, and a small bed. The pillowcase and chenille spread are pink. I really hate pink.

They let me have chalk and a green slate here. I estimate that I will be released from here in five years, if I can prove to Doctor Shiner that his therapy has cured me. Poor wretch that I am with no parents. Such trauma to endure. So, I am making plans. I write my plans on the slate, memorize them, then erase them before anyone can see.

WITNESSES

The life of a man named Harry ended on a Gambling Cruise Ship in the middle of the Gulf of Mexico during the month of December, 1993. The event took less than thirty seconds and was heard by hundreds of well-dressed, well-fed and very drunk partygoers. Harry was the kind of guy that passes through this world noticed by only a select few, changing some of those lives for the better, or worse, but having very little, if any, significant impact on the rest. That is, except the one person whose life he makes so unbearable that he is murdered. Harry's demise thus becomes the telling mark of an unremarkable life. Here is his story as told by some of the select few.

GEORGINA ROWE HUSKINS BOJANIAN: THE WIFE

It took me one year, three months, two weeks, two days and six hours to raise enough money to pay for the cruise on the *Santa Anna* Gambling Boat. Two thousand, five hundred dollars and sixty-seven cents for the cruise tickets, five thousand for my gambling purse, not to mention, but I will, the five hundred and fifty dollars I laid out for gambling lessons. I bet you cain't guess how many burgers I flipped and dogs I roasted, how many cokes I served, how many fries I incinerated to get that much dough. Come on, bet me, twenty-bucks and I'll show you my time sheets and pay stubs. I walked up and down Main Street from one job to the next in this goddamned below zero weather. The wind here in the Dakotas cuts through ya like a chain saw. Noisy and ripping. Most nights I go from my waitress job to McDonalds in ten minutes flat. Third shift for truckers to first shift for oldies and pimple faced kids. I got tired as hell some days. For the first few months the pain in my back felt like twenty hours of labor. I lost two that way. Two babies slipping from me and dying. I can still feel the knife cutting them from me. Ain't God's will, neither.

Yeah, you're right. It was all a front, a rouse, a game. I'm rolling high far as I'm concerned. Does that sound good enough for gambling talk? It was part of the lesson. The guy in the correspondence course said I had to "walk the walk and talk the talk of a gambler." I got just what I wanted, accomplished my mission. You think I'm just some white trash bitch? No down home blond bomb like me, five feet six, stacked, near fifty, looking thirty, can get away with what I got away with and be dumb. You see, I set out to kill Harry and get away with it. What? Nah, those babies weren't Harry's. But what I was hoping was that Harry would put a stop to my thinking I needed them. That maybe it could be just us. He sure treated me like that.

And let me tell you before I give you the whole story, the truth and nothin' but, that I aimed to do it real theatrical like. In front of about two hundred gussied up folks. I'd do it in front of the Captain, who could have arrested me for what Quincy used to call crimes on the highest seas. Hot-dog, me the main 'tagonist in the murder mystery. I intended to blow Harry's head off. I spent every night for the past year figuring it out, lying in bed alone, the cold night sticking to the windows. I could still smell Harry on the pillow next to where I put down my own head. He turned everything colorful for me. And soft, like I was special. He would touch me here and there and never hurt me; do it 'til I'd scream and he had to put his hand over my mouth and we'd laugh so hard the good, salty tears came. First time I ever cried happy tears. Can you understand that? Now, when I go to bed I know all I'll smell is stale ginger and sweat, like all the air was escaping from the world. That's what it's like now. Back home his pillowcase is still blue like the morning sky, with grease spots from his long hair. Harry had blond, curly hair that he let grow to his shoulders. He was always pushing it with his fingers. Tucked it behind his ears real nervous like. That was strange for a man his age. Fifty he told me once. He was sexy to me. And I guess to a lot of other women. I used to kid myself about that, trying not to be the jealous type. But Harry, well, Harry was like a magician. When he came near me, I could feel his heat coming to me, not like anyone else. I needed his touch all over me.

What he looked like? Taller than me, skinny, with deep wrinkles in his cheeks when he smiled. Blue eyes that matched his blondness. Shy, sort of, and nervous all the time. Inside himself like that actor that died in the fifties. Yes, that's him. Jimmy Dean. An old Jimmy Dean. I know Harry had lots of nice suits and shirts. But he always wore jeans and blue work shirts with me. It was sexy to me. Harry loved whiskey and coke and Winston cigarettes that he let just hang from his lower lip. He chain-smoked. I always had Southern Comfort on the table next to our bed, ready. I am an empty bottle now.

I killed him. I had to, don't you understand? I thought and I planned and I imagined how it would be, Harry's blood splattering all over some broad's fancy evening dress, his hair flying backward where the bullet comes out of his head. Bunch of old, rich farts looking for a quick lay. They cain't fool me with all that uppity music, like the kind they play at the dentist. Only thing worse is the whine of organ music and kneeling in church 'til my knees hurt. Country, that's music. Clint and Whalen and Johnny. Ain't no better songs then *I Walk the Line* and *Your Cheatin' Heart.*

Well, Harry put himself in a situation that made him a prime piece of meat on them cruises. Old ladies up the kajingkies, rich and begging for it. Harry, I gotta tell ya, was real good with them. Stringing them along, getting the goods and then he's outa there before they know it. And they're still loving the feeling. Just like I been feeling. Old broad's not enough for Harry. He needs a good woman. That's where I came in three years ago. Made me fall in love with him. By the time I got through with him, blowing my five thousand bucks for kicks, everybody on that cruise was gonna thank me for ridding the world of Harry Bojanian.

I know you're thinking who the hell is this character and why would I go to such far reaches to see him sink to the bottom of the seas like shark bait. Okay, okay, I'll calm down, start from the beginning of this here tale. Let me just give you the beginning picture. I described Harry to you already, the way he looked.

So you picture him. Now picture me. I'm a knock out. Picture Marilyn Monroe in that picture with that English guy. You know the one that was in that Hamlet thing? He's a prince in both them movies. But Marilyn's in just one. The prince falls in love with her, even though she's low class. You see both of us, right? Well, it's like a movie. A real honest to goodness love story.

Harry walked into the Crystal Dinner about ten thirty on a Friday night three years ago. It was early winter, November, so I was wearing a bright yellow sweater, tight, with white lace around the neck. I was trying for the demure look. I had just gotten my hair touched to shiny blond, again, like Marilyn, so it really went great with the sweater. I was on the second shift that had started at three in the afternoon. My feet were killing me already and I was bored to high heaven. Snow out of the Rockies prevented truckers coming through. I like them truckers, because they're funny and well, they sure do like me, too. So, anyway, there's Harry sitting at the end of the counter flipping through some book. His head was down, and his hair covered just enough so I couldn't see his eyes. But man, the lips and chin and the shoulders were enough to go tell Helen she had a telephone call. I wanted to get her out of the way so I could serve him. And when he put his head up, after I said "Can I help you, sir?" them eyes were all over me. And he says to me "If it's got anything to do with you, babe, I'll take it." So that's where it began. He was just passing through Bismarck, on his way to the coast to meet a cruise ship. What? Yeah, I guess that didn't make much sense. But I wasn't thinking about that then. And, man what a night. I fell in love right away. Harry made it back to Bismarck every couple months or so, and even if I saw the best-hung trucker come in, I swore them off. I had Harry and that's all I needed. We got married the second year. Harry always left me with lots of money, helped me get a swell apartment; even paid the doctor's bill when I had to have that D&C. I ain't got insurance working for a diner, ya know that. So this all went on for almost two years. Love, love, love Harry to the ends of the earth. 'Til one lovely spring day. He comes into town like usual, brings me a diamond bracelet, spends one wild night, and then tells me he'll always love me but, well, its been great and good-bye. Told me not to worry, that he'd take care of the divorce. Well, I'm sorry but if I cain't have Harry like he was, well, Harry just ain't gonna have no more fun is what I thought. And the more I thought, the more I knew it was like my destiny to get on that cruise ship he hangs out on and say good-bye right proper.

WAYNE ROMERO: THE NEW YORK POLICE DETECTIVE ON VACATION WITH HIS WIFE

I first met Georgina Huskins on board the Cruise Ship *Santa Anna*. My Mary booked us up with the special deal through her ladies group, the Sisters of the Sacred Heart. We'd been married ten years and never really had a honeymoon. Two kids later, me working the streets, studying for the sergeant's exam. When I finally made the grade, Mary presented me with this cruise. Our cabin was right next door to Georgina's, and she being a woman traveling alone, Mary thought it would be okay if we sort of looked after her. Me being a policeman and all and also I'm the protective type. Mary thought it was the answer to a prayer that Father O'Brien came with us, because such personages (that's Mary's name for influential people) got to have dinner with the Captain. We got to sit at his table the first night, have free champagne and fish eggs on saltines. Mary was glowing. I was happy to see her that way. You see, our kid Joey died three years ago. It couldn't be helped. He was born with something wrong with his lungs and it took him two years to die. Mary slept next to him every night of his life. Now, it's real great to see her happy again, like when we were young and in love.

She was sitting right across from me. Georgina, that is. If in all my years as an altar boy at St. Patty's someone would've told me I'd see an angel, I guess we'd have to take it outside. But there she was, my first angel, and boy did I believe. But, I'm a man too, not only a Catholic, so I, well, have these feelings sometimes. Mary says I have to control myself. That's what God wants unless we want more kids. One dead, one in high school now. A girl. Tammy. A real doll and good to her parents. Anyway. She had a gold dress on, and diamonds hanging from her ears. Her hair was like spun gold, like in the storybooks. She was sitting, so I couldn't gauge her height or body type all the way. So I started with the face, after the halo of hair. Blue eyes that looked at me and told me that the world was all mine. Purple stuff shaped her eyes like a female alley cat. Reminded me of those strays we used to knock around with when we was kids. White face something like Tammy's doll, you know, Barbie. Red lips that opened just enough so I could see clean, straight teeth and her pink tongue sticking out.

Like I said. I'm a man. The neck, oh God that smooth, long neck. I wanted to sink my teeth into her. The dress went down almost to the edge of the table. Her boobs, I mean breasts, must have been D cups, at least. She had a mole on the edge of the cleavage. Long arms with skin that shimmered. No hair on her arms, it looked to me. And red fingernails that matched her lips. She kept smiling at me, making eyes. What was I supposed to do?

I danced with my wife three times before Georgina asked me to dance with her. It was a slow dance with horns, I remember.

Music from when I was a kid, like my Mom and Dad used to dance to. I remember Dad twirling Mom around the room and us laughing. "Italians know that music is like the earth. It moves, grows!" is what Dad used to shout. Us kids would laugh and clap, laugh and clap. . . . Then Frank Sinatra started singing *Fly me to the Moon.*

What? Yeah, she did most of the talking. She was really interested in my work. I like that in a woman. Mary never asks me about my day anymore. She used to care about me getting killed. Made the Sergeant mad when we was first married, because she called the department to check on me four times a day. I had to tell her to stop it.

Well, can you imagine what it was like being in Georgie's arms? No, I guess you couldn't. Sorry. Her perfume was spice, ginger and lemons. It was a clean smell like an angel. Yeah! That's it, clean like hung out clothes in the sun or bright clouds. She told us all to call her Georgie. Like I said, I'm a man. Being a cop, you can imagine I see a lot, hear the worse sex stuff on the streets. But this was pure stuff I was feeling. And she was alone. And Mary told me to go ahead and escort her back to her cabin. I remember her exact words to me when we got to her cabin. First she touched my face, then she kissed my cheek, then she bit me on the ear, my left one. She pulled me into her room. There was champagne and cheese. I drank a glass, but I wasn't hungry, that's for sure. Then she said: "You know what I need. I know what you need. After, I'll tell you my story. It's about a man who done me wrong and he's on the boat." Well, again I have to tell you that I'm a man. And she was right. I needed that so bad. I was like a man that hadn't eaten for weeks and finally gets to the point that he can't anymore. But when the food comes . . . I know I shouldn't have. I know it now. She was an angel and what more can a man want. I fell in love. I had to. You must see that. And when she told me about the abuse she had endured. She even showed me scars on her legs. Her legs, for God's sake! Only an animal could do that to a woman. His name was Harry. He was on the boat and she was scared.

Did she what? Oh, sure, she told me all about it. She didn't even cry when she did. I think she's all cried out. She was married to Harry for five years. She loved him at first, but when the beatings started, she started to have different feelings. He only gave her enough money for food and hardly no clothes. Then she got pregnant. I'm not a woman, but I can imagine what it's like to lose it. Remember, I lost one kid. But he did it to her. Beat her and broke her nose once. Then he ups and leaves her. Poor kid. Then her mother dies. But her Mom left her a little money and so she booked this cruise, sort of trying to recover and all. But Harry found out and came after her. She said he told her he would kill her if she ever took up with another man. Can you imagine that? He leaves her and then comes after her like that. Well, like I said, I'm protective and a cop, so I talked it over with Mary and we decided that I'd look after her, make sure Harry didn't hurt her. She made me swear not to tell the Captain. She just wanted some peace. So, I said okay, anyway he hadn't committed a crime that I could see. Yet. We got real close, if you know what I mean. She needed someone. Sure, I think people can get close in just a few days. Why not?

I asked her to tell me what Harry looked like so I could watch him, make sure he stays away from her. She showed me a picture. I think Mary still has it. Well, the first time I spied him was at the bar about ten thirty the next morning. Drinking already. So I go over and sit a couple of stools away from him, just enough to get a good look at the scumbag. I sure can't see what could make a woman like Georgie marry such a nothing looking guy. Looked gay to me. All thin and stringy like someone hanging out in Central Park. Old too. Maybe sixty or so. Makes shivers down my spine like when I get a call that somebody's been shot and the adrenaline runs. That's how I felt sitting near the guy. I wanted to slug him.

No, I didn't talk to him. Didn't see why I should. I go back to my room to get Mary for brunch and Georgie's standing at our cabin door. She had a whopper. Her right eye was all black and blue, her lip busted. She said Harry came onto her early in the morning about three, promised not to hurt her, said he didn't want his scam on the cruise with the old white bitches ruined, whatever that means. I figured he was trying to hustle a few elderly ladies. There's a whole bunch of cruise followers that spend their lives stealing from the needy. Why Georgie let him into her cabin is hard to understand, unless sometimes you believe someone you shouldn't, especially if you loved them before. After he was in, I guess he couldn't control himself.

I was pissed. I wanted to go after him, bash his skull in. I couldn't arrest him. What authority did I have? She begged me not to do anything, but stay with her at night so she could at least sleep. Mary said sure that it was my duty. I did, for three nights. On the fourth night, before we went to bed, Harry was shot. The bursar found him in the Jacuzzi just when the guests were coming out for a boil. The Captain called me to confirm his findings. When I got to the Jacuzzi, they had turned the machine off, and man I never saw anything like it. It was like brain stew. Imagine it!

MARY ROMERO: THE DETECTIVE'S WIFE

It's been a lovely cruise, except for that murder. But, being the wife of a Sergeant, well, I'm used to it. Have you been on a cruise before? Well, the first night we got to have dinner at the Captain's table. Do you know what we had? French food. How elegant! Let's see if I can remember what we had. Oyster and bacon brochettes with a chili sauce to start. I close my eyes and can still taste that! Tangy and warm and crispy. Heavenly. Then we had blackened catfish fillets with dill mustard sauce and wild rice and fried sweet potatoes with powdered sugar and early peas and rolls. The rolls were still warm and fresh. I remember that smell in the mornings along Delancy street. I was raised in New York. Jews are the best bakers, really. And dessert. Pecan pie. I took mine with vanilla ice cream. I know, I know, I need to start watching my weight again. But who can resist the glory of such meals. I drank four glasses of champagne. Well, I couldn't refuse when the Captain just kept filling my glass. Such a sweet man. My aunt Lola would be perfect for him.

Georgina? Oh, yes, such a sweet thing. I'm so dark, being Italian, and she is so light, almost white. Not at all the classic beauty of my race. I'm Southern Italian like Sophia Loren, you know. We are quite full figured. Oh that poor frightened lady. She told Wayne that her husband was a wife beater and he was on the ship and he was after her and Wayne told me that he should do his duty and go protect that poor girl. I wasn't so sure. We were on a vacation and it wasn't his problem. I told him to go tell the Captain and let him take care of it. But Wayne's stubborn and never listens to me. I wanted to come on a trip like this for three years. I thought it would bring our love back. Father O'Brien was counseling us for a long time after my little boy died. I prayed and prayed and tried to go on with my life. But Wayne, well he wouldn't you know, pray. He won't even go to church anymore. I'm very involved with fundraising for the diocese in New York. It's been great for me and I do meet such nice and interesting people. I'm not home much. I even met a gentlemen that made me feel good about myself again. Not that I would cheat on Wayne. I'm a good Catholic. But, well, you would understand when somebody gives you hope. He even gave me a poem to read whenever I felt down. It's called *Hope*. I've memorized it. Would you like to hear some of it? Okay.

> We play the hand we're dealt
> Gamblers all in this old world.
> But one card stands out
> and it is you, Mary, the Queen
> that sees us through.

That's just part of it. Isn't it lovely and hopeful? He told me that the Mary was me as well as the virgin. He made me feel so good about myself again. His name? Joe Spadora. Italian. I miss him, you know. Oh, I'm so sorry. You don't want to hear my sob story. It sounds like a soap opera.

Wayne really tried to be a nice guy. He stayed with her day and night, it seems. Every time I'd ask him to spend time with me; he gave me her story all over again. But I understood. I always did before.

Curious? Sure, I got real curious about this Harry person. Wayne did show me his picture, made a big show of it like he was showing me a picture of the devil. I walked around the ship for two hours looking for him. I found him playing cards with three other men on the third deck recreation room. I sat at the far side of the room where I could see him head on. I watched him drink three glasses of brandy and smoke a cigar. He didn't look like a Harry and he really didn't look like his picture, not to me. It was the man in the photo, but somehow very different. Harry should be the name of a plain man. This was not a plain man. He was tanned with dark eyes. Black hair with gray on the sides made him look like Omar Shariff. The whole thing reminded me of *Funny Girl*. Remember when Nick took Fanny on the gambling cruise and then they got married? I suppose you're much too young to remember that romantic time. This man didn't look or act like a wife beater to me. I watched him for a long time. Hard to imagine that such a gorgeous man had his face shot off last night. He won the game, too. Nick, I mean.

I'm so tired of losing things. What do I mean? Oh, you know, death and then hope comes and then that dies too. What's the purpose of it all?

If there's nothing else, I do need to get to brunch. Sunday they go all out. All you can eat buffet. Let me know if you need me to explain more. Ciao.

Captain Hornblower: Ship's Captain

This is the first time anyone has been murdered on my ship. It's going to be the last time, you can bet your life on that. I'll put my money on the fact that this Harry was not killed for greed. It had nothing to do with gambling or money. I'm making sure the killer is found and that the reason is made very clear. I didn't spend twenty-five years of my life on the sea to have my reputation ruined.

Yeah, I knew Harry for five years. He followed the gambling cruise ships like sailors craving citrus, beriberi setting in. It wasn't winning the money that he liked. That was too easy for him. You took the dame chasing away from Harry, that game of chance, then I think he would have died. I would estimate that Harry got over two hundred of them in the sack, rocked this boat and their world. Not one of them ever complained. They smiled most of the time. He must have been something. Something to die for. I see how you're looking at me. That rueful smile. Quite attractive if I was younger. But, back to Harry. Harry died for love. I believe that.

I can't see the old broad Zelda killing Harry, not like that. A hit man? No, it just doesn't wash. Jealousy, hate, passion, revenge. Something like those. But who? That's it, the who. Harry was really a likable fellow when you come right down to it. I liked him, even missed him when he didn't come around that time a couple of years ago. That was the first time he ever missed the holiday cruise in five years. I thought he'd bought the farm, maybe died of cirrhosis. The guy drinks like a goddamned fish. Carried a gin and tonic around with him from morning until night.

A drink in one hand and one of those skinny brown cigarettes in the other. I never saw him drink anything else. But he never got drunk no matter how much his lady friends poured down his gullet.

Damn! Then he shows up for the Christmas Gambling cruise. He looked great. Like he had gained back ten years of his life. Tan, hair a little bleached, the lines in his face where like Sean Connery, you know, deep and sexy to any women over the age of fifteen. Harry also had this dimple in his chin. He had a prominent nose, that's the only thing that wasn't attractive as far as I'm concerned. But I bet the women liked that, if you know what I mean.

I had the stewards, only the guys, skim the Jacuzzi for his brains, now that the Coast Guard and you checked everything out. Man I'd like to see the gun that was used. They put the brains in a plastic bag, double wrapped with a black one so no one gets sick. Last thing I need is wailing and thrashing around here.

Funny though. They're celebrating on deck three right now. The wine and food are flowing. It's like those funerals they have in New Orleans. Celebrating Harry's life I guess. I sure would like to go like him. I bet he screwed a thousand women in his time. How many condoms do you think he used up in the last five years, what with the AIDS thing? Harry was a meticulous guy; always well-groomed, finger nails buffed and polished. A real *bon vivant* type. You know what they called Harry? The David Niven of the *Santa Anna*. I could write a book. Maybe I'll write it now that I'm retiring. Harry sure would make for a colorful character. There can't be many more Harrys left in this world.

The Comedian: Con-Dough

Funny thing happened on my way to the Lido Deck. Ba, ba boom! Sorry, that's always been my intro. Tacky, huh? But it gets them going and usually they're so soused, it don't matter what I say. I got my routine, I make good money, I like the water, and sometimes I even hit it lucky, get in with a fine dame. Georgina? Oh, yeah, can you believe a fine chick like her coming on to me? Hell, I say go for it when the opportunity arises, so I did. WOW! My papa never told me about hell fire and women. She's a devil that one. Makes pain pleasure.

But, you're right, there was something wrong with her. She was like, obsessed with something. Comedians sense these things. I study human nature. If you watch my act you'll see that I make people laugh at themselves. They like that. It's liberating. So I study the people on the cruise. I watch as they board, I select a few, then I follow them around. Get a good feeling for their flaws. And man, Georgina had something burning inside her. Always looking this way and that, like she was waiting for someone to attack her. I put it up to maybe a divorce, and lost love. But, God, who would leave a bomb like that. That woman made my head spin. Who needs drugs when she's around.

She carried a gun, I gotta tell you that. She told me it was for protection against her ex. He followed her on the boat and she was afraid. Said she had a restraining order, but left it at home. So, I'm sitting on her bed, you know after, and she asks me to follow him around, make sure he doesn't bother her. Well, I says, look lady, I don't want to get myself killed. Life's a joke and all that, but dead is just not funny, not even beat up is funny. So she says, well, can she just call on me if she needs help and I say sure anytime. Maybe she should tell the Captain what's going on. She says no, then the Captain would tell this Harry character something and then he'd really come after her and take the gun away. It was a little one, a baretta, I think. How she got it on the ship is a mystery to me. So, fine I say I'll keep a look out for her and we arrange to met about noon in her cabin. It was her suggestion. I still can't see what she saw in me. I mean, look at me. I'm the short version of Roger Dangerfield. I look like I got a worse thyroid problem than him. Bug eyes they call me. One thing comedians don't do is kid themselves. And I don't fall in love, you hear. So if you're thinking I had anything to do with the guy's murder, forget it. I ain't helping no dame out and end up in the big house. There is still a big house, ain't there? I use it in one of my skits and I like to be accurate. It's about a guy who cheats a gambling cruise ship out of millions of dollars over the years. He gets caught and goes rolling down the river. What? Oh, yeah, up the river.

No. I didn't see her the night of the murder. But I heard the shot, ran up to the Lido deck and there he was floating in the water, the water bubbling around him, red streams with muck spreading all over. I knew it was his brains. No clean shot that one. Someone wanted to blow his brains out if you ask me. I could still smell the gunpowder in the air. Metal and grease. You know that smell. Then everybody comes running, so I scadaddled. Figured someone would report it. I had a show to do at twelve and I had twenty minutes to prepare. There was one funny thing, though. They don't turn the water on that Jacuzzi at night. It's off limits until six am. Something to do with the water exchange or infection and cleaning the water. You can't be too careful now days with all the diseases going around. The Captain is real meticulous about those things. This is a prize ship.

Look, I'll be glad to help anytime, but I gotta go practice my act.

ZELDA DERSHOWITZ

They were playing a tango the night I met dear Harry. He taught me how to dance, how to laugh, how to drink mimosas for breakfast. He opened a whole new world to me. When Harry walked toward me the first time, I felt that lost ecstasy. Tall, thin reed of a man. He kind of leaned forward when he walked, like he was continually gaining momentum. He had one of those thin pencil mustaches, little pink lips that made my imagination wander downward, if you know what I mean. Dabbled gray hair. But you know, I didn't like his eyes. They were too penetrating. I used to dwell on every part of him, except the eyes. I would look at them, but never into them. Do you think I'm just an old lonely lady giving money to a handsome man just so he'll pay me attention? So what. I'd given Harry everything I had. That's what he meant to me. He was a Mensch. A Mensch I tell you! Do you know what that means? He had character. *Oi vey,* did he! In all ways. You think I'm dirty? So what's wrong with a little, what do you call it, hanky-panky between a man and a woman. We got the two right sexes, at least. He always dressed so well. Tuxedos he wore when we danced. He smelled like marshmallows and vanilla. Soft and clean he was. That's important in a man. So many men come to a woman when they're dirty. Like we're not worth taking special care for. But not Harry.

Oh, I knew Harry for almost five years. Been on a cruise every year with him. The first time I met dear Harry, he actually kissed my hand, looked at me like I was somebody, not just an old lady. You know he never asked me for anything. He was even real nice to my niece Maude. Poor thing, she was just not pretty. Homely little thing always slumping her shoulders. They danced, too, the first time. But, she never did come on another cruise with me. Except this one. She sure has changed in the last four years. She's a beauty, but so uppity. Intellectual type, you know. Went to Harvard, obtained a business degree and works on Wall Street. Imagine. I thought she'd end up a librarian or something. She's going to inherit all my estate because I don't have any other living relative, except oldies like me. She'll be a billionaire. I'm descended from one of the big industry owners in Germany. Guns is what my family has made for most of this century. I suppose you could say we are the suppliers of death. But somebody had to do it, *nein*? My father, he was real smart. He got out with everything before Hitler could take it. He hid a treasure somewhere in South America, since he did not trust the Swiss, and when the war was all over, well, he recovers it and invests in the stock market. A new fangled gadget he used to say, called the Univac. You and I know the rest of the story. Computers, computers, computers. They are almost as efficient as guns in killing the human spirit. A man before his time, my father.

I shall tell you a secret. Harry was only twenty years younger than me. I could have made him happy. He said he was ready to settle. He told me that he had become weary of running around and making nice, as he put it, to a bunch of ladies. I was the best and he chose me. I was going to marry Harry here on the ship before we docked in Cancun. I don't kid myself. I would have given him a five million dollar dowry and have him sign a prenuptial. I will miss him. As I said before, he made me laugh again. I was in Dauchua. I watched my family perish, at least the dumb ones who wouldn't leave like Daddy told them. Momma was one, and me, although I was little and didn't know any better. Daddy found me after the war. So, you see, he did the right thing after all. People like me look for happiness in every opportunity.

I have to go. I'm a pretty strong lady, but I do need my rest. I have Cabin 205. My niece? I haven't seen her much during the cruise, and surely not since Harry's death. She's probably in her cabin faxing to Wall Street and cornering the market in pork bellies or some other low thing. She's got not one romantic bone in her body.

THE MAN AT THE ROULETTE TABLE

I see everything that goes on and everybody that does it. Who's doing what to who and where. I'm the eyes and ears of this ship. They come here to gamble on a lot of things. Money's just the excuse for whatever they do.

How Long? Oh, shit man, almost six years I been standing at the gambling tables. Look, I might as well tell you now; they threw me out of Vegas, so I made my way to Atlantic City, but shit man, I'm not putting my head on the Mafia tables. Before they hooked me, I just got out. Got this job and it's all right, you know. Better than being a goddamned history teacher. Yeah, can you believe it; I got a master's degree from Duke University back in the sixties. Went antiwar and the whole cesspool. I like this boat, international waters and all that. I get this awesome feeling of freedom as soon as we pass out of national jurisdictions. I'm a free spirit.

The night of the murder? Yeah, I'll tell you everything I saw. It's a curious matter, to say the least. There I am calling the numbers and the colors, and I see this beautiful blond standing at the end of the table, to my right. She's just smiling away, looking all around at everybody, not really looking at anyone in particular. Hell, she was really distracting me. She's not gorgeous, but there's something peculiar about her. So, I keep glancing at her, then I asked Jonah to take my place, I was just getting too distracted. I go up to the bar and order a diet coke. We can't drink when we're working. Actually, we're not supposed to drink at all during the cruise because we're employees, especially the gambling crew. And I don't. Not since I started stepping along the big ten path, if you know what I mean. My great challenge is that I put myself right smack dab in the middle of what I want most in the world - a slug of Jim Beam. Where was I? Oh, yeah. So, I think I need to watch this blond woman, because something's coming down. We learn to sense the vibrations around us. That's how we can see whose cheating, whose shuffling the decks. The gambling crew, you must know, are the eyes and ears of the ship.

So, she stands there for about twenty minutes, smiling, smiling, then finally makes eye contact with this guy in a tuxedo. He's good looking, maybe about forty, dark, Italian looking, I'd say. So they look at each other, the guy nods just a little. I probably was the only person who could see that movement. Then they both take off. She goes first, out the double doors leading to the promenade deck. A few minutes later, he follows. Obvious to me, everybody else is too busy. When? About an hour before the commotion about Harry. You know, when someone found the body and started yelling her fool head off. Her? Her, I think, was Maude Dershowitz. Rich bitch. Sorry, but she wouldn't give a guy the time of day. Know her? Well, not really. But I've been playing the wheel for some six years now, like I said, and I remember she came with her aunt the second year I was here. What a dog she was then. If you look at her now, you'd never know she was the same person. She's beautiful now, but cold as a morning in Alaska, walks straight like there's a pipeline sticking up her ass. You can feel it when she comes near you. The air turns frigid. Turns me on, sort of.

Harry? Yeah, I saw them together a couple of times, drinking brandy and puffing away on them Cuban cigars. Both of them! But she's not his type and vice versa. Harry likes them older. They give a little, well, a lot. Maude. I can't see it. Not for love or money. No, Harry never gambled. It's too hard a way to make money. He sure stood next to his lady friends when they wanted to throw the dice, though. Made himself out to be their good luck charm. Touching their bare arms, old, white and wrinkled. Plunging necklines with glimmering diamonds. I couldn't do it. But, Harry, well he was one of a kind, and historically, the last of the debonair types. Poor guy, he never hurt anybody. Brought a lot of who-ha to the cabins of this floating casino.

About Con-Dough, the comedian, at least that's what he thinks he is. Well, he was having an argument with the dark haired guy, the one the lady signaled, about a half an hour before he came to the tables. Why is that odd? Con-Dough never talks to the passengers very much. He follows them around, makes fun of them, but doesn't make contact. Keeps to himself. Personally, I think there's something wrong with the guy. He gives me the creeps.

Maude Dershowitz

Scream? Me? Now who would have told you that? Do I look like someone who would scream just because I saw a dead man in a Jacuzzi? What? How did I know he was in the Jacuzzi? Well, well, word gets around, don't you know. Oh, sure, I was in my cabin most of the time. Oh, yes, I remember now. It was my aunt Zelda who told me the whole story. She had this thing for him. You know, the last fling and all. That was fine with me. No crime in a little fun when you're on your last leg. Good for her, I say. As long as she leaves me her money. I say that candidly, and why shouldn't I? I've spent most of my life doing her bidding. Maude, fix your hair. Maude, you're wearing too much makeup. Maude, please, do you think any boy would find a girl who takes business at Harvard attractive? She even paid a matchmaker to find me a husband once. I showed her. Do I look like an old maid to you?

Harry? You mean the man who was murdered? Of course I didn't know him. Do I look like the kind of woman who would associate with his ilk. Please, he likes the old needy ones. I am not old and I am not needy.

I do resent your prying into my life. Yes. I talked to him before. That was five years ago when I first came on this cruise with my aunt. But, even then I knew a pig when I saw one.

If you must know, I did graduate from Harvard with an MBA. Tops in my class and immediately was recruited by Janson, Janson and Smyth. I am their top broker. So, tell me, why would I have anything to do with this, this affair?

Report from the FBI Files on Harry Bojanian (transcripted and abridged) via computer transmission to Captain Hornblower

The prints from the corpse named Harry Bojanian were taken about two hours after the alleged murder. This was received and described by Inspector Adrieene Camus, a French citizen, acting in the capacity of unofficial advisor to Captain Hornblower of the cruise ship *Santa Anna*, owned and operated by International Holiday Lines, duly licensed to conduct business within international waters. The prints were clear, having been sent via computer laser printing. Analysis is here forwarded on this day December 27, 1993 as follows:

The prints are of a felon who spent one year in North Dakota's state prison for robbery. He has been known to take on several aliases to conduct alleged fraud on women for the purposes of extortion of monies. However, the FBI and other agencies have been unable to indict this person with a crime. Not one of the alleged victims of his schemes wanted to press charges, despite the evidence of forgery. One victim went so far as to tell an agent that "I want Harry to be whoever and whatever he wants. If he tells me he is DeGaulle, I would accept that. He can be DeGaulle, and I will be his Churchill. So what."

The aliases are as follows: Joe Spadora, Scott Wright, and Marvin Bernstein. He was indeed born in the United States, in San Diego, and given the name Harry Jenkins Bojanian. He is of Armenian descent and the Turks murdered his father during the Second War. He has always paid his taxes, was never audited, and served in Vietnam for two years as a Green Beret.

Agent Bernie Polanski

FLOATING BODIES

The body of the black man bobs five times before the hook pulls it to shore. I watch the almost feverish undulation of the water as the dead man goes under the smarmy water, then pops back up. Even though I am a great distance away, leaning over the railing of the Suwannee River Bridge, I can see where creatures of the water have taken bites from his flesh. He is naked, I can tell that, too. His butt explodes from the bubbles that are effervescent sheen and oily water, and the glimmering of once blood warm flesh is interspersed by deep gashes; serrated white flashes decorate the pink crevices. Flesh torn and spit out, back into the world of the polluted living. Metallic flavors engulf my tongue like thrush. Blue smoke fills the air in front of my eyes, and the smell of sandalwood crawls up my nostrils. I am chilled by my own sweat, but I know I must now walk down to the shore and look at his face, full to the flashing lights of whatever government agency has made it here first. I know more about this dead man than any human in attendance of his life or death, even his sweet Mama. Yet I have never met this man, this public figure once called *larger than life*, the *black John Locke* and even *America's preeminent judge of rightness*. So much for the words of scholars and journalists. Means nothing to us anymore. This man, this floating mother's son, I'm telling you, is accused of being a traitor to his country.

The hot August wind is like a searing blast against my face, even though it is ten o'clock at night and the moon is full. Lightning flashes from the horizon like the fires of prescribed burnings. Thunder pounds the sky and horsemen head toward this place. The water shimmers and sparkles with the reflection of the Bradbury moon, altered redder than the harvest moons of New England. Heat rises out of every pore of my body; every opening seems to release a liquid heat so that I must shake my arms as I make my way along the path where his body now lies, still face down. The smell of mushrooms inflates the air. Searchlights mark my way. They are starry torches of the crazed. That is good, since I must dodge the refuse of our humanness: shoes and underwear that wash up from the Suwannee shore, oil cans, old tires, dead fish, wood punctuated by worms, and steel. I am troubled by the floating of steel. How did it get here? How does it do that, defy the laws of physics?

I show my pass to the uniformed man standing over the body. He nods his head. His stiff brimmed hat hides his eyes, so that I see only a golden seal that brands his forehead. He does not know who I am, no one does, not by looking at me anyway. But I will explain that later. I study the man's uniform: a dark color, maybe navy blue, though the light is not bright enough for me to be sure, a gold-like stripe around the cuffs of the jacket and down the side of the pants, and on his upper arm a symbol of a badge with the letters FLA. I know that is the Federal Law Agency, an offshoot of the FBI, actually, a rival agency formulated by the man now lying on these once revered shores. How I love ya. I calculate quickly, (that is my greatest gift) that within fifteen minutes no less than seven agencies will each have something to say about this death. FLA, FBI, DEA, IP, CIA, SSI and FDLE. That's minimum. And don't think that each will not have a different "take" on who killed the man. Take. Everyone has a "take" on any subject you want to bring up. The point in "takes" is that there is no more Truth, only interpretations. Yeah, murder it is. Believe me, some will say it is justified. So is it really murder if it's justified? We used to believe that murder was, well, a crime, a sin, you know, *wrong*. Well, let me set my views on the matter straight right now, before I give you the whole story from the beginning. This guy really did bring this whole thing on himself. Once we look at his face and he's revealed, you'll know why.

The tall man in the black suit has finally arrived. I know it is a black suit because I know this man, too. He is the Medical Examiner from Washington, D.C. Amazing how he got to Florida so fast. It's almost as though the air parts for him as he walks down the embankment and towards the body. He says nothing. Nothing comes from the mouth that is no more than a deep slash across his white pasted face. He leans over the body, then hunches down, wiping his long white hair back on his head. I see blue veins and yellowed finger nails, all thickened from fungal disease. The wind blows his hair back over his forehead. The searchlight strikes his head, and it is as if Medusa has sprung to life. He reaches into his left pocket and takes out surgical gloves, thrusts his hands into the latex prophylaxis, then makes the sign of the cross, sad and dreary. He is not a priest, though he has often purported to be. It is all in the demeanor, sometimes. I see tears dribble down his cheeks, like melting snow from a rocky mount; and I am not surprised. After all, pride does goeth before the fall. And now it is time.

The ME, (I will call him the ME because his name does not matter to our present dilemma) grasps the body by the shoulder with one hand, scoots his other hand under the body and applies a sort of leveled action. The fleshy bulk turns slowly, and I am not sure it is cooperating, until the body is backed against the muddy earth. Begging eyes infect the sky. It is Roosevelt Able Stanford, first black (or should I say Afro-American?) Chief Justice of these United States of America, lawyer, civil rights leader of the bygone days, scholar, reported billionaire, and, according to CNN, ABC and whatever similar news messenger you want to listen to, a traitor. I know that this ME helped kill him and he will pay. But right this minute, I am here to tell you that Roosevelt Able Stanford is a savior. Or was a savior. Yes, we have no reincarnations today. He'd give the world to see the old folks now.

"Looks like he was shot six times in the chest and stomach," says ME, as he sticks his index finger into the gaping, raw holes. The white finger comes out clean. A bloodless man now.

"Sure does stink," says the FLA guy.

"That happens being in this shit pool of a river for more than twenty-four hours," says ME. "We'll wrap him up and fly him back to Washington. You're not to talk to anyone but your Commander, do ya hear me," he says with a down home accent. Down upon the Suwannee River, far, far away.

ME pushes up into a standing position. A quick breath of stale air opens his suit jacket. His torso is wrapped by a bulletproof vest that is like a backward turtle shell. He snaps the gloves off, makes a ball and flings it into the river. The ball comes undone, separates into two, flutters down like an eagle descending to feed, and softly spreads on the water like supplicating hands. Go and be a part of the pollution. ME looks at me, nods and turns away, heading towards his helicopter. He doesn't know who I am, either. There is the assumption that since I am standing in the area, I am acceptable. I love being innocuous. *Innocuous*. The first time I read the meaning of that word, running home from school and promising myself to learn ten new words a day, I felt the exhilaration (new word) of being. There I was, just seven years old, poring over the *Is*, beginning on page 561 of Webster's, when it came to me; this was my life, this is how I would be somebody: be innocuous: "not likely to give offense or to arouse strong feelings or hostility." I've spent my life getting to this point. It is amazing how much one person can accomplish by living behind the scenes. Not like being a Chief Justice of these United States of America.

I watch the cobalt blue sky suck the helicopter away and I suddenly feel abandoned. Then I turn toward the shore and the body that has been transformed into a fat black bag. It is being lifted into an ambulance. Doors close and the automobile heads up the embankment and into the hallowed night. The sounds of horns roll in from the world beyond, trumpets announcing civilization. I walk to the lapping edge of the river and put my right foot gently into the water. Wet warmth permeates my skin. My left foot squishes into the sandy mud and I begin to slip. When I look down, I see that three scorpions have risen up to join me.

Good or evil, yen or yang, vice or versa, I mumble to myself. I will return home, to an apartment that is always cold and only a dime throw away from the Potomac. The place where I live is wrapped by the foul and misty breath of the homeless of today and the ghosts of yesterday, who whistle the tunes of Hooverville. It is a sound of doom. Good-bye America, how are ya? I am homeless, too, but far from helpless, since I still can whistle through my teeth.

My name is H.E. DuBois, better known as Dubbie to my colleagues and friends. To the FBI, CIA, DEA and all the other supercilious agencies, I am known as just H.E. They do not know that I am Dubbie. But, as H.E., I am in great demand. I am the world's expert in linking the mind's intentions, whether thoughtful, thoughtless, subconscious, buried, regressed, split, sublimated, incarnated, or whatever, to any piece of paper written on, touched, scribbled on, be it plain paper, notepad, legal pad, steno pad, post-it pad, prescription pad, the most sophisticated legal document, love letter, hate letter, whether you talk common law, civil or criminal law, or no law. Write it down on touched paper and I can read all intentions, down to your attitude, political leanings, hates, loves, inner longings. You cannot hide once you write just one syllable, even one cursive or typed letter. I am a Forensic Document Examiner, *par excellence*. Words on paper are my passport to another person's life.

The social contract is supported by pieces of paper. Remember that so you can understand the full impact of my story. I had been called in by the Deep Seven (composed of one member from each of the government agencies and supposedly cooperating parties) five weeks to the day after Stanford had risen to the highest lawmaker's post. That was four years, to the day, ago. The Deep Seven's charge was to investigate any and all real or supposed subversive groups, functioning within and/or outside the U.S. borders. Let me tell you at the start that each thought they could use me, manipulate me, make the words mean what they wanted. They surely did underestimate me, old innocuous. Dividing and conquering doesn't take might. Now, RAS (that's the secret code for Stanford and very original) I will tell you now, was never a traitor. I repeat: He was to be our savior. Now he's dead.

But, why do you think the Deep Seven really called on me? What were their motivations? The fact of that multiple solicitation puzzled me, at least for a while. Then bodies started to bob up in all the waterways, and lakes, and tributaries, man-made and natural, within the confines of the legal parameters of Washington, D.C. By April of 2021, as I was two months into my work with the Deep Seven, and having gleaned much from the documents given me, eight bodies floated through our capital. Every last Friday for eight months a body floated and bobbed its way along the capital estuaries. At first, and according to the authorities, there was no rhyme or reason. One each month. Remember, I am a calculator. But I am much more. I know from the paper, the touch. So I managed to insinuate myself into the previous lives of the dead. I got hold of pieces of paper they had written on, pretending to be a bill collector, insurance auditor, or even a medical claims adjuster. Funny how those words instill fear in us. I want your money! All of the dead floating bodies had one thing in common. They were in some way related, by blood, to each of the justices that sat on the Supreme Court, except RAS. Uncle, distant cousin, sometimes three times removed. One of the now dead bodies had recently arrived from Sicily and was a member of the Cosa Nostra. We don't hear much about that organization now, but believe me, I've touched many of them. I know them. Why weren't the justices themselves murdered? Blackmail? A warning? Yes, a warning. Because dead bodies are ugly things, especially the way these people were killed. Three were children. There is no mercy. And a warning of what, you might ask? I suspected, but was not sure. Five months went by with nothing happening. No more floating bodies. It was five months of torment. It was to begin again, but I was not ready to stop it. I certainly couldn't tell the Deep Seven and then expose myself. Besides, not one of the Deep Seven seemed a truly trustworthy human being; all men, all buzz cut hair, all white, all muscle-bound. I have to tell you here, I saw them, but they never saw me. It wasn't necessary since I only work with paper, and I exchange my reports through secret computer files. Never paper files. Never. Then the eight Justices were murdered. Floating down the river. There was one more to go, nine old people, and RAS was last. But I didn't expect him to die so soon.

Walter Lippman once said that it is the job of the journalist to give a "picture of reality on which the citizen can act." Who said the picture has to be true. We've heard it all before. It is propaganda, although, in all deference to old Walter, I don't think that's what he meant. But we ought to be more careful when we make pronouncements. They can be taken to mean many, many other things. By December, things had gotten out of hand. Who could you believe anymore? Roosevelt Able Stanford, I was convinced, knew what was happening, was interred in the only branch of government that could restore, well, sanity. No other black robed citizen took a seat where the dead had butted heads. So the bees hummed and the banjos strummed. Our country was divided, pragmatism reigned, there were no Truths, and we were now on the verge of revolution and only RAS was perched on high. But, can I start from the beginning of who I am? That's the only way that you can help me restore balance.

In the spring of 1999, I was fired, okay down sized, from a position I had held for almost twenty years. "Just pack up the things in your desk and leave. It's much better if we do it quiet like" said Stephen Smythe. I was second to the top editor for Fields Publishing. We represented and published the works of the best selling authors, both fiction and nonfiction. Anyway, there I was, cut adrift.

One morning about two a.m., as I stared at the darkness that was my bedroom ceiling, contemplating my fate, counting the memorized water-stained squares, it came to me. Start your own business. I wasn't a writer of great, good or mediocre literature. It just took too long to get a point across that way. Sometimes five hundred pages go by and you make one point. So I sent out fliers and business cards, and advertised in the local newspapers: *Have you ever wanted to write a letter to someone . . . the letter that puts down in written words all the stuff you wanted to say to that person? Like: hey you, you hurt me when you. . .. or I love you because . . . I've always wanted you to know. . . . Let me do it for you IN JUST THE RIGHT WORDS, TO GET JUST THE RIGHT EFFECT.* And, yes, I refused to dabble in insults or threats that could result in violence.

Well, if anyone ever proved that Americans have a lot to say to each other but couldn't because they are functional illiterates, I did. The calls were ceaseless, endless. I had more work than I could manage. And a funny thing happened. Well, it was scary at first. When my customers told me what they wanted to say, and I started writing, it was like I was them, their lives flashed into me. I knew everything about them, their desires, angers, hates, fears. I became them. My business grew, I wrote a book that sold over five million copies, and I was invited on the talk show circuit by the stooges, Geraldo, Oprah, and Larry. I didn't go, because anonymity was necessary for my success and safety. Remember innocuous? I wasn't even on the dust jacket. It was great! For a while. But could I sleep at night knowing so much? I was going crazy. Every time I touched a piece of paper with words on it, I saw the person who wrote it. I flashed into them. I couldn't stand it anymore. So I decided to vanish, retreat to the mountains before I went insane, totally ballistic, postal, ended up sing singing.

No doubt my special gift was triggered when I started presuming to think for someone else. To write the words they should have. I was manipulating other people's lives. Despot! I called myself, laughing. Where did this come from, originally I mean?

I was born in South Florida, on the border of the white world and the Big Cypress Reservation, the only child of a one hundred percent Seminole Indian mother who was raped and impregnated by a white man, whose goo became me. My mother told me the whole story when I was five, that instead of the Musicians of Bremen that I was longing for. " Rest your head, little eagle," she had said, "because your Ma has to tell you something about why you are special." I know you will say it's wrong to describe rape to a young child in vivid living color. Especially of a mother by a mother who always wore vermilion instead of red, whose form seemed clothed in the sun when she worked in her garden. A mother worshipped by the child who knew no other. But, there was a point to it. And the point had slipped away until I had started writing those letters. Even when Ma died, I didn't remember. I should have. She died defending her property rights on the shores of the Okeechobee. Her heart gave out dead in the path of the bulldozers sent by the twenty-four judges, circuit, regional, county, state and supreme. It was an old trailer, pushed up against the dried scrub, alligators waiting for a childhood snack. She had dared to stay off the Reservation. She, descended from Osceola, lines drawn straight to Chief Billy Bowlegs. I remember the burning trailer, Ma screaming at me to "remember your gift. Born in violence to know violence." She had yelled it in the language of her ancestors, Calusa, way back when. A rejuvenated tongue like hands on tree bark.

Do you think I went into this whole Deep Seven thing to exchange rage for revenge? Go play psychologist somewhere else. That couldn't be further from the truth. I love my country. It belongs to me.

When I wrote the first love letter for my new business, I suddenly remembered talking to animals, leaning out of our trailer window, nurturing quails at the edge of the scrub, never fearing the moccasin, and gathering crop eating grasshoppers without cages. *Whoot* and *peep* were part of my young soul's vocabulary. I had the intuition, the knowing.

So, my business took off, I could read the souls of the loved, beloved, the vulnerable and the hated. And desires put in words by me on tangible paper became reality. This was the point at which I began my experiments. I wrote a letter to Elliot Asimov Channels, the richest man in America. He had gluttoned the American economy, made pigs of us, and stole one good name. This is what I wrote: (I knew his bodyguards or secretaries would get the letter first, so I included them all): *Dear Mr. Channels, bodyguards, secretaries and other hired underlings: Give the money back.*

Within three months, Channels had disbursed (I love that word) most of his cash, stocks, mutual funds, and credit holds over valued companies. I was convinced. I had the power of the word. Just one more example, lest you doubt my abilities and thus miss the full impact of my story. I wrote the following to all owners of the major professional football teams. *Item: please have your players recite one recently passed law during half time.* The nation was captivated. If a football player cared enough about his country to know the laws, then the people were going to imitate that interest. Trading cards, even for baseball, "re-played" a law, rather than player statistics. The American people became enamored, and even began to debate the pros and cons of the laws recorded on the cards. Collectors' items. Talk about a free society! That is what I did in my vanishing period.

It was fun until two things happened. Roosevelt Able Stanford became Chief Justice of the Supreme Court and the Deep Seven activated their underground move against the reading Americans. History tells us that governments, democratic or not, really fear the masses. When they are educated, watch out! I guess you could say I had created a historical event. A dialectic, so to speak. Fear no chains. A sports fan understanding the Omnibus Spending Bill, well, that is frightening, awesome. Riots broke out, because now debates that usually took place in Congress, or even at town meetings, spilled over into the public arena. It was Greece and Rome all over again. Gadflies all over the place. So who was going to stop it? Overt or covert law? Ha, there's the rub. I sided with Stanford. Go overt yourself.

I could feel the Deep Seven when I held a newspaper that printed the words CIA, FLA, FBI or any insane use of the alphabet. Their seal was on the message. So, I decided that I was born to use my powers for good. I am the fiddle player in the town of Breman, still longing for the old plantation with trailers all in a row. I wrote to the Deep Seven's overt organizations (they open all their mail) and simply willed them by words to contact me: *use me*. They did and thus I was hired as part of their underground organization. I was the subverter of the subverters. But I didn't bank on Stanford being murdered so quickly, before my work was done.

Dear FBI (etc.), I wrote the following morning, October 12. *It has come to my attention that you are not utilizing my skills to your fullest advantage. Here is what I can tell you about the death of RAS. You are the perpetrators, all of you, and I will name you to the world. On Monday November one, 2024, the day before elections, please read the newspapers of every major city in the United States. Do not try to use the Internet. It is touchless.* That, I was sure, would scare the bejeebies out of them. (or is that really bejesus?) What would they do between October 12 and November 1? I was counting on their reaction. Really, I dictated it. They are so predictable.

Deep Seven started an all out war with each other. They overted. I had them just where I wanted them. By October 15, twenty-four agents had mysteriously died, their bodies thrown into the Potomac. Why not the Suwannee? Because the river running through our libertine town was a much more effective signal. It was all a simple run around the bases, a joke about whose on first. Everyday from October 15 to November 1, I advertised my intention to Deep Seven. Section D, Sports, page 10, in the *New York Times*, for example, a five by seven ad that read: *go get 'em boys.*

It was all too easy being a despot. I promised I would always be benevolent. None of this "benign neglect" stuff. I would opt for progress, depend on the enlightened few.

Deep Seven continued to call on me. Touch the ad; tell us whose doing this. We're killing each other. No shit, Popeye. What could I tell them? Should I lie? Absolutely not, I'm all against lying. I'm for truth with a capital T. *I have traced the documents to an internal mole. He is among you. I make out the letters D, H, U in the name at this point.* That message sent seven times and sealed by my hand, signaled the end. By the end of October, the Deep Seven no longer existed, at least for their original purposes. Whoever was left in the cabals were left to sadly roam the world.

I knew that the election of 2024, presidential and others, was to be great theater. The usual two parties presented candidates, with six other recently formed parties offering sacrificial mimes. Socialists, Marxists, progressives, knight riders, secessionists, and even a deconstructionist party. Political advertising is expensive. The media has one message. The pamphlets of days gone by had touchable words. What are you reading? Words. My old publishing house had gotten wind (through me) of H.E., and I very easily convinced them that the H.E. and the me of the five million plus books sales were one and the same. So, they graciously published my pamphlet (anything for a buck), and called it a chapbook for literary marketing purposes. The publisher sunk huge amounts of money in advertising and promotion. By November first, sales were up to ten million, an all time record for a sixty-page chap entitled: *Internal Revelations.* It was purchased mostly by the voting public for the price of a burger all-the-way. $5.99. Sales went up to eight million, my contract gave up ten percent, and my rights were to last for four years. Anyway, what the hell, I could change the contract by written suggestion. Well, I was rich, rich, rich.

Internal Revelations hit the public on the simplest level possible. It talked constitution, rights, property, liberty, tolerance, and really said very little that shouldn't have been known already. I paraphrased the great works on popular sovereignty all the way from Plato to Jesus to Locke, Montesquieu and Thomas Jefferson and finally ended with RAS's seminal work, *Against the Tide,* which rivaled only the legal briefs of the still respected Justice Brennan.

I suppose it sounded original and unique to the voting public. Americans had journeyed so far afield. Dismal education. Now, the true body politic learned from baseball trading cards and professional football players. I had brought back the civics lesson, in substance if not form, for form always begs for the morality play. My publisher soon notified me that we had gone into second printing.

On November 2, a new president and a host of other representative personages were elected. All eight parties got people in, with the majority going to the grand old two, but they certainly were learning a lesson. Chapbooks may be the best hope for civilization.

So, here I stand, listening to the swish of the water in the Suwannee River, planning the future of my country and watching ME fly up into the clear night sky. It is a bright and starry night. I can make stories come true.

WOODSTOCK

Professor Woodstock died just as the fifty-year-old scotch trickled down his esophagus. But the sweet, burning effect of the liquid was not the cause of celebration. Woodstock had waited more than ten years to open the bottle. Ten plus grueling years of writing, rewrites, revisions and, worst of all, the vitiated derision of his colleagues throughout the academic communities of the South. Woody, as his students called him (referring to a particular body part), used his philosophy classes, Epistemology 101 and 102, as his sounding boards. Yes, the aged golden nectar massaged his throat and he thought, finally, that it had all been worth it. There would be embossed words, *his words,* on white paper, all encased safely between leather bound hands: scripted gold lettering *shall* give his name as authority. The Enlightenment be damned! The smell of new pages would assault the pores in his nose. He tasted that wonder already in the punctuated scorch of the alcohol. These were not his imaginings. The letter had arrived in the early morning post. His *magnum opus, St. Thomas and the Great Heresy,* had finally been accepted for publication.

Now, it had been calculated over the years that less than half of Woodstock's students had any idea of what he was talking about during the endless hours of his classes. The droning nasal pronouncements put many to sleep, others dreamed of the green budding of youth, and some took notes diligently, hoping for extra points on his now infamous examinations. *Explain Nietzsche's power of will.* Those students who did have at least a little idea, or glimmer, as you will, of Woody's philosophical ramblings, simply believed that their teacher was mad, because all philosophers were anyway. *Nothing comes from nothing.* Then there was the two per cent or so who reveled in the certainty of their dear professor's coming greatness, who followed Woodstock with their eyes, necks slowly turning, as he paced to and fro, traversing the large, high-ceilinged classroom with measured, tapping footsteps, and his cologne leaving waves of stale air in his wake. The bass voice explicated the definitive laws of the universe, as echoes bounced off the shiny, hand-carved wood that held the history of the mountains. *Morality is not relative!* boomed the five-nine stork, clad in all dark brown tweed. To be taught epistemology by the man who wrote a *magnum opus*, the great Woodstock! It did sound dignified. Words just couldn't express the anticipation of this potential connection with greatness. But Woodstock was mentor to no one.

So it was with shock, confusion, and relief that the news of the professor's demise was received by the students and faculty at Mountain School for Boys. Woodstock had been a colleague, a philosopher who had died an untimely death. Much mileage could be extracted from such publicity, noted the pragmatists on the board. It was expected that *The Great Heresy* would at least make Mountain School famous for a while. "Heart attack," the official post mortem read, although some expected murder, rather hoped for murder, as it would at least throw some excitement the way of the boy's preparatory school. There were no sports at Mountain School.

But one living creature knew the truth of Woodstock's death. The Professor had not been alone when his very last breath clicked loudly and involuntarily in his throat, catching him by surprise. The last being into whose sparkling eyes Woody looked, and who looked back, was one Immanuel Cat, named by the Professor as a negative charm for the completion of his opus. Cat, a gray and white alley puff, was named after Immanuel Kant, the philosopher of reason and love, but not out of admiration. The professor utterly, unequivocally, categorically despised Kant for what he believed was the denigration of biblical postulates. Only St. Thomas Aquinas was held in greater contempt. Ergo, Woodstock hated cats. Useless creatures. The *summa* of all things. *It would seem that not all moral precepts belong to the law of nature.*

Vulgar creatures sent by God to spy on mankind. "Judgmental least ye be judged," Woodstock was known to say, often. And on this point Woodstock was reduced to deductive ramblings. It is enough to say that Woodstock hated all things that smacked of the Cartesian scheme of the world, whether backward or forward in the curves of history. He had been sent to Harvard by a very wealthy and influential father, one who had made a fortune selling lumber extracted from the Blue Ridge Mountains, strip mined, ran moonshine, and collected rent from the People of the Hills. The nineteen thirties had been kind to father Woodstock, for he knew too much about certain members in Congress. After all, he was a good southern Democrat, who voted for both Harding and Hoover, unbeknownst to anyone. The son returned from Harvard not only a political conservative, but a nineteenth century Fundamentalist. "All things derive from God," he said while thumping the Bible. But his father refused to send him to "preacher school." So, Woodstock made the formation of young minds at Mountain School his mission. Mountain School was situated at the foothills of the Blue Ridge Mountains, and from there Woodstock was never to venture. The world, he said, was tainted by sin.

Like his namesake, who had accepted near poverty in exchange for thought and spirituality, Immanuel Cat did not despise anyone or anything. He saw the world in terms of a higher purpose. Cats are, after all, sent by God. A Truth. Immanuel already knew that the *opus* was never to be mentioned in the annals of philosophical thought. Woodstock had become so fanatical in his rage against the sins of the world, so mean-spirited and bereft of love, that he had succeeded in pushing an angel off the head of the pin.

Marilyn Woodstock, nee Pennywise, had been the most beautiful woman to grace the social evenings at Mountain School, at least when she first married and came to live in the town of Cave Hollow. Her flowing red hair padded just at her waist, forming a sheeny halo around the top half of her body. Forest green eyes, flecked with yellow, burst from the white face piercing and devaluing the most famous Civil War portraits hanging in the school's prized museum. She danced when she walked, ethereal, really angelic, and the scent of wisteria preceded her coming. The skin on her arms held no pores from which black hairs could grow. Her flesh was always just right warm and she brushed against you like your own mother when illness or grief had shattered your world. Marilyn was all comfort. Why she had married Woodstock was a great mystery. Most people guessed it had to do with money and political promises. She had no close friend, man or woman. After about two years in the Cave, as the students called their seat of knowledge, she had become sullen and ashen. The sparkle may have gone from those eyes, but who could know. Mrs. Woodstock, nee Pennywise, ceased looking into the eyes of others. Rumor was that she had contracted leukemia. And nothing could be done to help.

Immanuel Cat had made his way to Mountain School three months after Marilyn took up residence as the Professor's wife. Professor Woodstock considered himself a "gentlemen," so allowed his wife the pleasure of the feline, despite his distaste. Actually, he began his course Epistemology 101 with the words: "I am spiritually a southern gentlemen. I expect each of you to be the same."

The young men who were sent to Mountain School at the tender age of seven came without benefit of intellectual rigors. Their years of consciousness included blasting in biblical interpretations by preachers who spoke in one simple tongue. *Sin, sin and more sin.* Most of the boys could shoot a carbine better than they could read. But their parents, all of them with family money passed on for generations, had an inbred hatred for the public school system. It had become an "evolutionist conspiracy," ready to rot the souls of their children. Mountain School was there to keep the sullied world at bay. There was no Freud. There was no Darwin.

Before Professor Woodstock died on his first and only day of celebration, he did leave a message for the world. On a piece of paper, which he clutched in his left hand (the glass that still held some scotch was in his right), was written the word *Cant*. His prized student, Jack Bullet, was first to find the Professor and thus removed the paper from the stiff hand (and downed the rest of the scotch). For weeks afterward, that one word consumed Woodstock's philosophy students. It was a matter of great epistemological debate. What did the Professor mean?

"*Can't* breath, *can't* breath," was one theory presented by Donald Smith, his arms thrust wide, the freckles of his face popping into great prominence, eyes glowing with laughter, his breath spewing tobacco spit. He had been humiliated many times by the great Woodstock.

"*Can't* is a word interpreted by red neck ass holes like you, Smith," argued John Buck.

"You *can't* know what he meant by *can't* if you weren't there to validate that he really said that word, or meant it. There is no foundation for that knowledge. We *can't* know nothing," said Jack Bullet.

One shy and withdrawn student by the name of Esterhazy Buchanan mumbled the word *recant*, but was shunned by his classmates. Esterhazy was fifteen. His upper body had been tortured by acne for more than two years as a result, he unwittingly believed, of his lonely night excursions into growing manhood. Little Estee had uttered the final words of the great debate, and the story had been picked up by a national magazine and printed in a back page section called "Trivial Pursuits."

Immanuel Cat had sat at the feet of St. Thomas, Kant, Faulkner, McCullers, Barth, and even Buber, just to name but a few. He remembered silently wandering the hills of North Carolina with Mr. Wolfe one spring day, the pedals of the pink dogwood gliding onto his upturned face and catching his whiskers. Cool angel wings. Cat was of great comfort to all of them. Marilyn Pennywise left Mountain School two weeks after Woody's death, carrying in her purse a letter from Woodstock's publisher. She had found it under Cat as he rested on the window sill on an early spring day while the pink azaleas danced with the yellow forsythia. It read: *Philosophical Press has been purchased by the Carolina University Press. We regret to inform you that we do not deem your work of merit sufficient for publication. You may wish to try elsewhere.*

THE GOD PARTICLES

My Dearest Tommy:

I have written you every month since you left on that black train. I can still smell the oily smoke that spit from its belly. Do you remember, Tommy? Thirty-two years makes eight hundred and eighty-four letters. On the last day of each month, at sundown, I screwed up my courage, and wrote you about the lives of those you left behind. I wrote in restaurants, coffee shops, bookstores, bus stops, libraries, wherever I happened to be when the appointed time came. I was always alone, I made sure of that, so that I would not have to answer questions about who you are (or were). I kept writing even when the war was over, because they never told us you were dead; not even presumed, dear brother. The letters never came back to me. I now know where they went, where they still rest, unopened. They will never be opened; they are God particles and will be returned only when the end of your life on earth begins. So, my dearest, I can now rest, no longer having to wait for a reply. It was you that I saw climbing the steps to *Sacre Coeur* last evening, while I moved forward quickly to avoid the assault of pigeons. I feared for my eyes, their beating wings were like trinkets at the *Mardi Gras*. Tommy, you finally made it to Paris.

My thoughts were never far away from you. Never in all these years. It has all moved so fast and I felt that I knew you only by hearsay. But what is time really, but a space between before and after, atoms that refuse to gather to energy. Have faith that I have always lived all sides of my love for you. That's why my letters told you about every part of my life; my insides and outs, as we used to say when we were kids. That's how I kept our love alive; all others were as sterile as surgical instruments. So, Tommy, I gave you the only thing I had to give when I could not touch you, keep you safe anymore. Every time I wrote you, I gave you a little more of me until I was empty of my solitude. I have no more particles of me to give, so luck was with me when I saw you yesterday. What joy!

I will give you my last thoughts, the last good God particles, and hope that they will dust the night sky and my life will now begin for real. I was never nourished by your vanishing.

We are all born to a mission, I believe, a plan that God sets for us whether we know it or not. I knew mine the day I set eyes on your baby face. I remember all of your faces, Tommy. I was born to take care of you, and I failed the day you jumped on the moving train and headed out to Vietnam, to serve your country and not our lives together.

Let me go back, please, to what we were back then. I ask myself too often why you were tall and I was short; you dark red, me so light that I hated the blue veins that pulsed on my neck, my hair so blond it was white before I had a chance to age. You were so tall and strong, and people were amazed that it was me, the sister, who used up her young life looking after you. Oh, Tommy, it was because you were a goddamed pathological liar. . .pants on fire, brother. Mom laughed at your lies, thought you were cute, like your landing in trouble and jail was like eating and breathing. Expected. You were a born liar. But I loved you more than she did; I was the one got you out of jail, paid off the sheriff with more than money. Did you know that? You were too young to go to Nam, but you betrayed my efforts and ran right smack into the line of fire.

Let me tell you this story about how we were born. It's Mom's story; long dead Mom smoked and drank herself to death because of Daddy and you. I bet she would have had a wonderful life had I been an only child. I'm sorry to tell you that. Please don't feel guilty about it; you've been redeemed by your own absence; it is me that received the punishment. I had to watch her slide into hell. And here's what she told me. Make of it what you will:

"I knew the very moment I conceived Tommy. Not like with Saucy. No, with Tommy it was real slow and enjoyable and I knew the moment he came to life; and when he came out to the world, well, he just kind of slipped up on me and I was feeling no pain. He pushed his way out of me when the moon had risen full over Whiskey Bay and Daddy went out past Henderson to catch gills and perch. With Saucy, it was like somebody shot hot water up my legs and into my vagina. I wanted them to just go ahead and kill me. It was raining and I had to push her out of me. Tommy went up into my mind, like them tent preachers talking about Jesus coming into them. I carried Saucy high and Tommy low. Children are that different right from the start."

I'm glad you never heard that story. I'm sorry I did. I have enough bad memories to inhabit a dead planet.

I'm sorry, too, for what may seem my extraordinary fragments of thought. Be happy, you will not have to read them anymore. (Tommy, I know you received my letters and ignored me for my diligence). As I said before, this is my last letter, number three hundred and eighty-five. How many God particles does it take to make a whole star, or plug a black hole, or stop a meteor? What would Ptolemy think of my theory on convergence?

Many times, too many, I imagined you lying in a rice paddy, dead in the Mekong Delta. I forget that mirages exist only in deserts. I stopped watching television for fear I would see your body dragged through the straggle of alleys that was Ho Chi Minh City. Then I studied maps of southeast Asia until I could answer any geographical question as to place, time, economic status, food sources, population, elevations. . .on and on, just so that I could imagine you alive and still part of that patch of our world. How inevitably sad that your vanishing deprived us of a shared reality. To love, brother, is to smell, touch, taste, and hear the aging flesh of another. I laughed at the thought of your big freckled faced, red-haired body on top of a tiny little Vietnamese girl. Did you leave any babies behind, Tommy?

I almost wish I could tell you that I am dying, and that's why I am writing this last letter to you. I don't believe you'll buy the God particles business. But I'm not dying. I'm as healthy and physically fit as anyone sixty years old. I could have raced to the top of *Sacre Coeur* steps and tackled you if I had thought it necessary, if it would have brought you back to me. But I didn't and I won't. It's time I go home and leave you to your new life. It's all been a lie, and that's not surprising is it Tommy? Was your not coming home a lie? And who are you? My memories of you are fiction, false, failures.

When did you get to Paris? Did you escape? Where are the bones you left behind as evidence of your existence? I ask questions still and I know you will not answer me. But I have to know. See! I make myself a liar like you: You arrived in Paris in 1971; you escaped, killing three guards, wrapped your dog tags around the neck of one of your platoon buddies whose body had been blown to smithereens by a landmine, then changed your name to Charles LeDuc, telling everyone that your father was in the Resistance (your Cajun French came in very handy). You are that famous writer who will, no doubt, win the Pulitzer Prize as the story you told of your father (a lie!) touched the heart of a morally weary world. Congratulations.

There, that is my story of you. Now I know that you are safe no matter who you really are, no matter that you can still lie like our Daddy.

I mail this letter now; the sweet glue from the envelope will linger on my tongue, only to be washed away by Mom's favorite gin. Stamps are thirty-three cents now, Tommy, so you know just how much I've really invested in you over all these long, calcified years.

Go with the God particles,

Your loving sister, Saucy.

GENETICS 101

I'm a forty-year-old orphan. Once an orphan always an orphan, they say. I was shuffled from one foster home to another from the time I was something like five years old. I never did remember anybody that could have claimed me by blood and eventually forced myself to stop remembering anyone who would have claimed me by love. But I done good all the while, dreaming that old American Dream. You know the one: a mom and a dad and a biff and a sandy and a prince and a muffy. That is, until the day I met Charles Edward Mican the Third, started my search for Helena, and placed that ad in the personal section of major newspapers: *Helena, please come home. Mother bought you a new dog. His name is Prince. We love you. Charles.*

On the morning of September 5, 1998, I flipped through my appointment calendar for the coming two weeks. The words "boring" and "stress" summed up my life. I suppose it comes from measuring a life by committee meetings with blank faces who'd sell you for a stock option. I kept thinking about lists. The best hundred books of the century, the best movies of the century, the most influential people of the century, the best things I've accomplished with my life. What were the best hundred days of my life? I thought backward through the last year. No best days. Then I looked forward to dull days that I already knew would pass into one more day, and on and on to the sixth day running into the seventh day and then the eighth of July when I noted for *my* record, if not the century's, the meeting in which I was assigned to report on our West Virginia plant where a worker had been killed. It was my birthday. Maybe that's why I had ended the notation on my calendar with an exclamation point. The guy who died was only twenty-eight.

My mortality has always been important to me. I am afraid to fly. I schedule business flights as early in the morning as possible, only because I am barely conscious then. I figure it's better than boozing up. I had scheduled the West Virginia meeting with the manager of the plant, whose last name was the same as about ninety-percent of his workers. I tried real hard to avoid surprise at family resemblances when I inspected the plant for safety problems. I truly wanted to help. Did I see Norma Rae or Billy Jean?

No, but in the afternoon I met with our company lawyer. I thought lunch would have been nice, since it was my birthday, but I really detested that guy; pompous, squeeze the injured worker for all they were worth, find a loophole in their insurance portfolios and worker's (he insisted on calling it *workman's*) compensation policies. Not illegal he would tell me for the hundredth time, but unethical, I would tell him for the hundredth time. The dead worker's family got all of fifty thousand dollars.

The next morning, I quit my job as risk manager for the large textile manufacturing company. My job had been to make sure internal company policies lined up to federal laws. I worked with that bastard lawyer for five years making sure we covered all the loopholes so that when someone got hurt or killed, we could dodge the law. Racket or what? So, who was the unethical one here? Answer: me. It just all of a sudden got to me. I felt like a slug. I saw the guy's wife and kids waiting outside the manager's office. I did the American thing; take your job and you know what with it, here's my pink slip, the table's turned, thanks for the use of the hall and I'm out of here. I walked out, all my working possessions in a cardboard box labeled *Office Supplies: Distribute According to Policy.*

And I went home, thought about the best one hundred days of my life again and came up with one. Today. I found the date in my notebook and labeled it *My New Life*. Then I called a lawyer friend who, after three scotches, had once suggested that I go into business for myself, be a sole proprietor. I figured I'd have at least twenty good years left.

Harold Stein met me for supper that night. He's single, but please, Harold can only be a friend. He's too short for me. Anyway, I had bouillabaisse and hot French bread and he had a salad with no dressing and no bread. So I knew nothing, *nothing* could come of Harold and me. But Harold is really smart, and he convinced me. Within two weeks I had a license, found an office for three fifty a month, paid twenty-five dollars for a guy to paint *Charlotte Boone Investigations* on the door, and waited to start my investigations, to find answers for the less fortunate, whose lives had been tortured by loss, damage, vilification, threat, stalking, or accident. I knew I was looking for redemption, but hell, what's it all about, anyway. I sat in my green leather chair that creaked and kept me awake. One week went by, I stared at the telephone, drank pots of coffee, and gained three pounds from stuffing Whoppers and fries in my face. *Nada, zilch, rein*. . .Then he walked in. All blue eyes, sandy brown hair, square jaw, full mouth, baby smooth skin that would grow a beard by five. He smelled like lilacs and I thought of moonlit nights. It was nine a.m. and he talked until two that afternoon. I ordered hot pastrami sandwiches in and started a new book of schedules while he went to the community restroom down the hall. I taped his story. Here is the beginning of my first case. And as Hazel used to say, boy it was a doozy.

Transcript of Charles Edward Mican, III's story, August 2, 1998, as typed by Private Investigator Charlotte Boone:

CB: Okay, Mr. Mican. Just tell me why you've come for help.

CEM: My grandfather told me that "Loss is just a sojourn of our lives." I've always believed that and so has my family. That's why we have endured for so long, you see. That's why I'm the third of somebody. Anyway, it's all about my sister, Helena. Helena Bouffard Strand Mican. Great name, isn't it? My whole family, all of them, always thought that Helena was crazy. That belief goes back to when she was only twelve. She had such unusual ideas. Now they think that she's dead. But I don't and that's why I've come to you. Harold is a friend of mine. He recommended you.

CB: Who is included in your family?

CEM: Back then, when they thought Helena was crazy, it was my mother and father, our sister Hannah, and me. I'm the youngest, Hannah's the oldest, and Helena, well she's the middle child.

CB: I see. Please, go on with your story. I'll just interrupt you when I need to, you know, fill in the blanks.

CEM: Surely, Ms Boone, I understand completely. I will try to be thorough so you will not have to. Now, to continue. Helena left home when she was nineteen years old. She had just received her BA in social anthropology from Cal State. She came home often the first year, then communicated only in letter form for ten years after that. My parents received a letter every month. The letters always arrived on the first Monday of the month. They were always typed. I brought some for you to look at. They were never signed. There was always a salutation: "Love from planet earth, Helena." Every letter included a photo of one of her friends, classmates, boyfriend, and even homeless people. The letters would tell us that much, but never names.

CB: Did you recognize anyone in the photos?

CEM: No. The letters were quite specific as to where the people fit into Helena's life. Categories. They always seemed to be standing next to someone, but there would be no one there. For example, look at this photograph. The young man is standing in front of a lovely scarlet bougainvillea, his arm is raised and turned as though he were holding someone around the shoulder, but there is no one there. Where that person is supposed to be is a little yellow post-it. See this one. On the post-it is typed the worlds "Helena not available for photo" and a stick figure, as a child would draw when that awesome power of brain to hand coordination evolves .

CB: Huh? Okay. . .so where did the letters come from? I mean, didn't you try to track them down?

CEM: Well, of course. But there was never a return address and the postmarked locations changed with every letter. By the time we would try to locate her, there was no trace of her, and then here would come the next letter from another place. There was never a listing in any directory for her with any of her names, not even initials. Nothing we tried turned up anything. Ten years and one hundred and twenty letters have gone by.

CB: Who is this *we* you're talking about?

CEM: Oh, my family hired several private investigators over the years. Father handled it completely, as he did all things. But the investigators could find nothing.

CB: That seems odd, don't you think?

CEM: At first, yes. Yet, it's all true. No trace of Helena. Anyway, if I may continue. This went on for ten years. It drove my parents to distraction. For Mother, I think it made her somewhat insane. She talks to Helena in all kinds of nooks and crannies of our home. She even bought her a dog a year ago. She named him Prince. My father went crazy with anger. He believed Helena was trying to get back at him. I think he grew to hate her.

CB: For what?

CEM: I do not know. Honestly. I was only twelve when it all began. Father hired several detectives to find her, but nothing came up. He paid a great deal for them. Then father died last year.

CB: May I have access to the detectives' files? By the by, how's your mother today?

CEM: Surely. And Mother has become what her psychiatrist calls "nonfunctional." Aren't we all, though? Before you ask further questions: My sister Hannah does *not* want anything to do with this business of Helena anymore. She does not want to know when, where how or if Helena shows up in the world. Hannah has simply become immune to the loss. She calls Helena a virus. As I related, I am the youngest of the Mican children. I cannot pull myself together about Helena. I have become somewhat obsessed, Ms. Boone, and I need to exorcise Helena. I can only do this by knowing.

CB: You were just going into your formative years when it began, Mr. Mican. It is quite understandable that you would be affected. It must have been very traumatic for you what with your family's, well, concerns.

CEM: Yes, I think you do understand, Ms. Boone. Thank you. Today is Helena's thirtieth birthday. I want to take another chance at finding her. I've put aside what I call "Helena's Search Money", so I will spare no expense that is reasonable. Will you help us?

It was at that point that I turned the recorder off. I had what I needed of the story, at least for the time being. Less is more, they say. I took notes from the rest of our conversation, after I accepted the job and Mican offered me two hundred dollars a day and all expenses even vaguely related to finding Helena. I promised to give the Mican family a full written report of my progress weekly. Charles Mican stipulated that he was to be the first person to see the report. He would decide who else would be given information. "You're the client," I said. Mican the Third was twenty-two, a Harvard engineering student, rich kid, and smarter than you'd imagine at first glance. I believe in hidden motivations. I always get a itch that starts at the small of my back when people lie to me. Sometimes I just can't stop itching and have spent a fortune on calamine lotion.

Years of butting my head against concrete walls taught me lots of short cuts. Cut through the crap is my work ethic. Mican had left a metal box filled with Helena's letters, so I spent the first morning on the case listing all the places postmarked on the envelopes, then took out an ad in the personal columns of twenty-five major newspapers. The ad read: *Helena. Please come home.*

Mother bought you a new dog. His name is Prince. We love you. Charles. I gave my phone number as the place to call, and waited. I studied the photos; all the people were nondescript, ordinary, blended Americans giving me zero leads.

A week went by. Nothing. Mican brought me the detective reports, so I spent my time reviewing those. They contained the usual stuff. And I might add very halfhearted attempts, when there was any at all, at finding Helena. Either they were screwing with the rich, or the father didn't care. Motives, I thought, as my hand headed for the itch at the small of my back. Only two detectives had bothered to call Cal Tech and interview Helena's roommates (she had three in one year). According to the roomies, Helena was quiet, never bothered to make friends, and stayed away from the dorms for weeks at a time. Helena was described by an anthropology professor by the name of Dorfman as brilliant, introspective and cool. One detective had interviewed several male classmates who went ballistic about her looks: "Raven hair, tall, black eyes, full-bodied, orgasmic." All in all, the files included fifty interviews, none giving any hint as to what happened to Helena. Only one report gave a clue that I could use. Helena had applied for a grant with the Anthropological Institute of North America to study the results of poverty in the South Central United States, specifically, the Appalachian Mountains.

I called the Financial Aid Department at Cal Tech, pretended I was a loan officer at a large bank's adjustment division and convinced a Ms. Hollman, Administrator of Grants, to give me information on Helena Mican. Helena had received a grant and presumably headed for Virginia. The next morning I punched the record button on my answering machine, rented a car and headed for Roanoke and the Appalachian Mountains.

"Excuse me," I said to the most beautiful Afro-American lady I had ever seen. "I'd like to see Professor Simpson." She had those almond shaped cat green eyes that poets laud over, a full vermilion mouth that smiled untold secrets. She was a mixture of the pyramids and Appalachia. A Nubian nymph of the hills.

"He's quite occupied at the moment. Can I ask you what this is in regards to?" she breathed with, well, a voice like a mocking bird in the magnolia tree. I am known to fit in just about anywhere I go. The fate of an orphan living a tenuous existence.

"Yes. Please tell the dear professor that I am here to talk to him about Helena."

"Helena? Just Helena?"

"Sure. Try that. If he doesn't get it, then I'll further expound. Okay?"

"Sure thing, honey," she said with a laugh. I smiled back at her.

I backed up and sat in a hard, wooden chair that was missing the left arm. I watched her sway through the doorway marked *Social Anthropology, Dr. A. Simpson, Head.*

She walked out quickly. Her face had taken on a serious tone, her lips were pursed, and she gently pulled the door closed saying "yes sir, fine, I will, yes sir." She turned to me, shook her head, rolled her eyes, and slapped both of her hands over her mouth. She was suppressing wild laughter.

"What? What?" I asked her.

"You sure did make his day. I think he turned white as a sheet. Made my day, I tell you,"she said.

"So he knows Helena then? Can I talk to him?"

"I'd bet he knows her, otherwise he wouldn't have reacted that way. "

"What way is that exactly?"

"Scared shitless. My, my, my. As grandma used to say, I do enjoy making the white man jump every once and a while. And no he won't talk to you."

"What did he say?"

"Said he didn't know anyone named Helena and that he had committee meetings all day. Told me to get rid of you."

"You're not very loyal, you know," I said.

"Please. This man doesn't even know who I am half the time, he's so wrapped up in himself. "

"Do you know anyone named Helena?"

"No. But I've only worked at this job for about four months. And that may be it. This man is freaky."

"Freaky?" I asked, sitting on the side of her desk, trying for the casual, let's be chummy effect.

"Yeah. Look, I'm supposed to be his secretary, right? Well, I can't go in his office when he's not there. I can't touch his files, he has his own phone line, and he sneaks out to the post office instead of just putting his stuff in the out box like everybody else. We all know that these academic types justify using the university to pay for their personal mail. Secretaries talk."

"You've been a big help, more than you'll ever know," I told her, holding my hand out and getting a firm, warm handshake.

"Whatever," she said.

The university library was real big. I tracked down a reference person who plopped down five large tomes in front of me. I picked up the book on top of the pile: *The Effects of IntraMarriage on Successive Generations*. Genetics 101. Mendel and the Peas, the Princess and the Pea. Don't marry your sister, first cousin, or even second cousin or your children will turn out looking like elephant man or acting like Ted Bundy. Second book: *Appalachian Families and the Curse of Generations*, which detailed the same genetic postulates but brought them down to an understandable level. Banjos in the hills came to my mind. The third tome was authored by our friend Professor Simpson of the publish not perish set. The book was called *The Shame of America: The Hidden Life of Incest*. The fifth and sixth books had too many graphs and arrows and whatnots for me to understand, even when I turned to the last pages, hoping that there would just be an end to the story, the who done it of genetics. Library files showed no entries under the name Helena Mican, or any of her other names. A nice library assistant, a young man about fourteen it looked like, made a copy of the introduction to the professor's book for me.

"How much?" I asked, digging my hand into my pocket.

"Just go," he said, "this place shouldn't charge for knowledge. Besides, I'm a unionite. Screw them."

"Good luck," I practically yelled at him. Then I gave him my card. "Call me one day, I know the bastards real well. I owe you one."

I took a long stroll through the ivy-covered paths of Virginia College. The dogwoods were in bloom and I thought of my favorite writer, Thomas Wolfe, then realized that I was in the wrong state. Well, literature is a state of mind anyway. Cool air pushed my hair around my face, the scent of azaleas brushed my nostrils, and an incantatory sound inflated the air. The clanging of bells from a tower told me the truth: it is all in the blood. I sat down on a dark green garden bench that faced the entrance to the social sciences building. The professor would be returning some time, his dark head clear in my mind, an image from the dust jacket of his *magnum opus*. I watched robins and jays dance in the trees. A bunch of daffodils had emerged from a clump of soil to the right of the bench. Daffodils that persisted year after year, fertilized with bone meal. It is in the bones, I sighed. Dem bones. What kind of life had Helena been living for the past ten years? I did not believe that she was dead. No, Helena was still blood and bones.

He was bustling my way, his brown jacket open and flapping like a bat. I could hear the tapping of his heels as he struck the sidewalk, the puffing of his breath as he expelled forced air. The head was a black waving mass of stringy hair knocking greasy tendrils at the air. As he moved towards me, I could see his face was red up to his eyes, the forehead was white as though his body stopped oxygenating at exactly the point where the crease in his nose split his upper head from the rest of his body. His eyes were lead-colored like the gauzy remnants of life, crowned by one bushy eyebrow slashing across his face. If the eyes are windows to our souls, truly, professor was an empty vessel. Are soulless people anthropological anomalies? Do they have lineages? Descents? Species identifications?

"Excuse me," I said, stepping in front of him, my legs spread. I had worn jeans and cowboy boots.

"Professor Simpson, I presume. Thought I'd catch you out here. Save both of us some time."

"Who are you? What is it that you want?" He spewed the words at me. He moved up to me, his body bent like a gargoyle, his eyes wide and meant to scare me. The smell of camphor was nauseating.

"I'm trying to find Helena Mican. She received a work study grant here about ten years ago. She was to study family lineage in the Appalachian people. Can you give me some information please. Her family is looking for her."

"I do not know a Helena. I'm sorry," he said, his jaw clenched so that the words came out in growls.

"But surely you must have known her. You've been on staff here for longer than ten years."

"They come and go, miss whatever your name is. I must have had hundreds of graduate students work under me. I do not remember them all."

"Oh, Helena was a memorable person, professor."

"Really? And what makes a person memorable? Especially graduate students. They're like little piranhas thinking I would just give them the knowledge I've worked so hard to attain. I could care less about your little Helena."

"Perhaps if you just look at her picture here. Please, just study it for a moment and then tell me yes or no. You're an anthropologist. Memory is what we are, isn't that so, professor?"

He took the picture. I expected him to dash away from me, spit out hate, fumes trailing after him. But he pulled in his bottom lip, the upper teeth clamping down so hard that I could see the blood being expelled from his skin.

"You know where she is, don't you professor? Mendelian inheritance was your specialty in the field of social anthropology. Was Helena a good student? "

He moved sideways like he was falling, so I caught him by the arm and helped him sit on the bench. I realized that he was a very old man. I had endowed him with vigor that was temporary. He held the photo in his right hand, his left hand was now fisted and pushed into his mouth.

Brother Charles had given me that photo of Helena on his second visit to my office. It had been taken before the disappearance. The whole, intact family was present. There were no post-its. Helena was a striking figure. She stood taller than the other four people in the photograph, smiling as though she knew the secret life of whoever looked at the photograph. Her head was like a helmet of chestnut hair, the face was large and controlled, the eyes wide and dark, almost black, her nostrils flared, reminding me of a mare after the act of copulation. If birth were expected from a union with Helena, it would be awesome. On her right stood her mother and then her father. Mrs. Mican was short, very blond, with red lips and light blue eyes that were once predictably happy. She was beautiful. Father Mican simply had the look of the crazed and dissatisfied. Helena was his spitting image. On Helena's left were Charles and sister Hannah. They looked just like their mother. Mendelian inheritance. Helena apart from mom and siblings. Just like daddy. How did that happen?

"She was the smartest student I ever had," he snorted.

"Tell me about Helena, professor. Where is she? Let me find her."

"She can have no life now," he squeaked. "Please, not now. Leave me alone."

"I can't leave you alone. Her family needs to know."

He pulled at the front of his white shirt, buttons flew outward into the fine air like fireflies catching the moonlight. He fell to his knees, taking me with him, my left arm clasped in an iron fist. I felt his saliva attach to my cheeks, the hardness of the sidewalk on my head, and then a heavy weight fell on top of me. I smelled camphor and freshly released urine, then I felt a wetness on my leg.

"Helena," he whispered. "In the mountains. Mangled roses. Save her."

I pushed myself up, using my body as a lever to pry the professor off of me. He rolled over onto his back. The eyes that I thought were soulless had now become merely the rheumy old eyes of a dying man. His tongue quivered, hanging out from his opened mouth, lost in foamy spit. I looked around to call for help, but saw an empty campus. The world had slowed down, quieted but for the chirping of the birds and the grinding of a far away chain saw.

"Professor Simpson. Where is Helena? Where?"

"The roses . . .in the moun. . .cave. . .her fate. . .hide. . .." He was still.

I searched his pockets, grabbed a set of keys, jumped up and walked quickly towards the social sciences building. I hoped that Nubian would be out of the office. It was lunchtime. I found nothing in professor's office that could help me find Helena. On his key ring was a tag with his name and address and medic alert. Diabetic. He had had a stroke and once lived on Maple Avenue. I made it to my rented car within a few minutes, found Maple on the city map I had purchased on my way into town, and headed out.

Maple was upper middle class America, perfect for a movie set portraying the torment of rich families in crisis, the theme being suffering is relative. Professor's house was a two story Victorian, hidden from the street by vaulting azaleas, lilacs, and a few other flowering bushes I could not identify. The driveway was empty, there was no garage. Somehow I knew that professor had been single.

I parked about a block away from the house, strolled into the back yard and let myself in through the back door. Fear, apprehension and dread took hold of me. A clock ticked. I was in the kitchen and from the high hanging window came a sheer light, like illumination that fell from a tunnel.

I tiptoed through the dark house to the living room and then the dining room, the eak, eaking of my footsteps in time with the ticking. I touched the walls and felt ice. Professor's study was large, ceilings high, meticulously encased by mahogany. Two sides of the room were dominated by spiraling shelves of books, the third was hidden by forest green curtains, the fourth was a huge marble fireplace, all reminding me of the Fall of the House of Usher. A large desk sat in the middle of the room facing the fireplace. None of the drawers were locked, but I found nothing that would help me. I sat looking towards the fireplace, wishing for warmth and fire. Above the mantle was a beautiful painting of the mountains. In the middle of the painting was a dark scraggly entrance, as though a huge claw had scooped out a passage to the earth's core. The entrance was surrounded by cascading red roses and a shaft of sun hit right at the entrance; it was like the pure light that had sparked the first life. I moved closer, pulled a heavy chair to the fireplace and stood on it, pushing my face toward the picture, squinting. A piece of branded wood spelled the words: *Mican Mining*. I pulled on the right side of the painting opening it to a shelved cave stuffed with papers.

Chambers of Commerce in small southern towns are usually located on or off of a Main Street. Mars, Virginia was no exception. I found a parking place in front of what looked like a renovated five-and-dime store and presented myself like a tourist to a woman who must have been older than the hills. Her nametag announced her as Betty Watts, volunteer.

"Good morning," I said loudly. "May you please help me?"

"What?" she shouted at me.

"I said I need help!"

"Oh, help, yes, okay. What help can I give you, young lady?"

"I'm looking for information on a company called Mican Mines."

"Oh, dear. They's been long gone. There's no more company at all." Her voice and head shook, orange lipstick was smeared around her mouth, and the watery blue eyes signaled mild distress.

"How long has it been closed?" I asked.

"More than forty years, I'd say. Maybe fifty years."

"Can you at least tell me where it was located?"

"You don't want to go up there, young lady. It's far up and very dangerous. Those lands are still private. There's been no more mining going on."

"That's okay. I just need directions," I said.

Miss Betty reached under the counter, spread out a map, and with a red marker drew a circle around a large green spot. "Here, follow this winding road out of town until you get to the circle. Don't go on them lands, I'm warning you. "

In less than a half an hour, I sat in my rented car figuring how I was going to get through the barbed wire fence and up the mist covered mountain. According to Betty's map, the mine entrance was about two miles away.

I tore my jeans right at the edge of my butt trying to get over the fence. The woods were cool, with a soft breeze whispering that interlopers would be *punished, punished*. I concentrated on human footsteps following me, or the hissing of snakes. I had been walking for almost an hour when the sudden barking of a dog made me stop. Sweat poured down my back. "Wolf or nice doggie?" I said out loud.

I sat on a downed tree and cursed my decision to come into these woods, take this case and damn it all, believing I had the guts for investigation. Reverie is a great thing, but not when the wind tells you that punishment was at hand. *Hurry, hurry away* was what I felt, and then the barking of that dog was coming toward me. I jumped over the tree and headed away from the sound.

I ran through a thorn bush and into a clearing. A house was about twenty feet away, tucked into the side of the mountain and wrapped in brambles and vines that cascaded down and around the wooden pillars of the porch. Red roses and orange trumpets danced in the now gentle wind. The entrance into the house was black as coal. I hesitated then heard the barking behind me. I ran to the doorway and yelled "help me, please I'm coming in!" I rushed in through a screened door and slammed it behind me. I whirled around to the throaty voice of a woman who sang: "Prince, shut up and go play."

I would have as soon felt the cold steel of a gun at the base of my skull as look into the eyes of Helena Mican. She had not changed from the picture of more than ten years ago. Her wild black hair was long and reached down to her waist. A pink ribbon held it back from her face just at the crown of her forehead. The skin of her face was flawless, shining in a ray of sun from a window, contrasted by a room that was otherwise dark. It was the wide strangeness in the eyes that I kept coming back to as I inspected her. Her neck was long and smooth and a large goiter pulsated like a man's Adam's apple. She was dressed in a long, cobalt blue dress, with sleeves that delicately touched her wrists. She had unusually large, brown hands. Her feet were shoeless and dirty.

I leaned on the door jam, trying to control my breathing so I could speak. I closed my eyes and said: "Helena, you're alive."

"Of course I'm alive, silly," she said, the singing voice like a Homeric siren. "Come, you must be tired. Prince does frighten. But he is harmless, truly he is."

I sat in one of two wooden chairs in front of a small table. What must Helena's life have been like all these years here, I thought, wondering how much I should ask, fearing that in this person was perhaps madness and danger. I scanned the room and saw nothing that could be used as a weapon.

"You're Helena Mican, aren't you?" I asked.

"Yes, I am Helena. How long it has taken for someone to find me," she said, looking straight into me, smiling. It was as natural an act as breathing.

"Your family has looked for you for ten years, Helena. They have been crazy with worry."

"Have they? Well, I'm better not found then, right? I wouldn't want to disturb their peace."

"Why did you disappear? Is someone after you? Are you afraid of someone?"

"I carry a disease, Miss, what is your name?"

"Charlotte."

"Charlotte. What a lovely name. Charlotte and Helena. It's very poetic don't you think? Both names of poetic heroines that were lost. Dead, crushed on the stones of life, blood splattering all over the world, like atoms in the cosmos. They were diseased!! That's why they are dead." She growled the words through her teeth, her hand clenched into fists.

I pushed back my chair, ready to take my chances with Prince.

"I'm sorry," she said in her siren voice, "I get very upset when I think of what could have been if I hadn't been born me."

"Have you been out here alone all these years?" I asked.

"Oh, no. I'm well taken care of."

"Professor Simpson?"

"Yes. He is why I have survived."

"Helena. Am I your first visitor?"

"Oh, no. Sometimes Professor Daddy lets me have a visitor. But they only come one at a time. Didn't Daddy send you?"

"Ah, yes, in a way. And he wants *you* to tell me about yourself. So we can become friends."

"Really? I've not had a real friend."

"Why did you come here, Helena?"

"Didn't Professor Daddy tell you?"

"No. He said it would be good if you did."

"Really?" she asked. She was silent for a while, her gaze focused on the window. It was four thirty and I had about two hours before dusk and a chance at getting out of here.

"I'm diseased. I cannot leave here because I might spread it to the rest of the world."

"You look fine to me," I said. "Who told you that you have an inherited disease, Helena?"

"I discovered it when I came here to work with Professor Daddy. The Mican name. The inheritance that would be my fate."

"You think that you are the child of your father and his sister, don't you?"

"Yes. And I am defective. That was my study and I found out all about my family when I came here. The Mican tragedy. My mother was not my mother and I really had no brother or sister. Hannah and Charles were lost to me. I never did understand why I was so different from them until I came here." Tears formed in her eyes and fell down her cheeks. She didn't wipe them away. "I can never have children, never love. So I came here and Daddy Professor helped me. Better to hide away. I've been happy here."

"So alone, though, Helena."

"I have Prince and the mountains."

"Your mother has gone crazy since you left, Helena. She was

still your mother, raised you, loved you. What difference does it make about your birth? It's all accident. It's what we do after that's important." I was surprised at my own compassion.

"But you're not defective," she whispered.

"Neither are you. I don't think what you found, what Professor Simpson fed you, is at all true about your family. Someone is setting you up, Helena. There's a fortune waiting in Mican Mountains and you're the one that needs to be dead. Professor thought he was protecting you, but he was just delaying the inevitable. Come with me, let's be sure. I don't think your mother was your aunt."

"But why didn't my Professor Daddy tell the truth?"

"I don't know that. We may never know," I said. I chose my words and then decided that the straight truth was best. Too many years had already been wasted. "You're father died a year ago, Helena. Your mother is sick with your loss, your brother hired me to find you. I have. So come with me. Take your life back before somebody else finds you. I'm afraid that they will kill you."

"Why should someone kill me?" She asked

"Look," I said, " Professor was sending a signal to someone all these years with the letters. It was a cry for help. I guess the job fell to me. Somebody wants tons of money that your father has left in trust. Helena, he has left you all of these mountains that come under the Mican name. The greedy ones are the deviants, not you, no matter what we find out. I know them. Come with me."

I heard the squeak of the screen door, saw the sudden shift of Helena's gaze and felt the gun on my neck before I could turn around.

"She's not going anywhere, and neither are you."

"Hello, Charles. What did you do to Prince?" I asked.

"He's sleeping. Every little doggie likes a piece of meat. Helena. You're looking well. Hardly changed all these years, little sister of mine." He laughed, the Harvard ambiance gone, the craven brother, my client, had emerged. The scent of lilacs was gone. I smelled sweat and madness.

"How long have you been planning this?" I asked.

"Oh, about five years. I waited for just the right moment, for just the right stupid, yet resourceful, detective to lead me to Helena. I love being right, don't you?"

"Yeah, but I guess I can't always smell shit right under my nose," I said.

"No need to be crude, my dear. This should be a joyous time, the reuniting of brother and sister." He removed the gun from my neck and walked over to Helena.

"You haven't changed a bit," he said, caressing her wild hair with his left hand.

"Why? I don't understand," whimpered Helena.

"The most common reason of all," I said.

"Shut-up!" Charles screamed. "What the hell to do you know about this?"

"You hired me, remember? Let me give you my report now, okay Charles, then Helena can hear the whole story. She's the rub, as they say."

"Please, I want to know," said Helena. Her voice was in control.

"Go ahead, then. My last gift to you, dear sister, you'll be dead soon, anyway."

"It was the Professor that sent the letters to your father as a way of signaling that you, Helena, were alright. They were in cahoots. The other detectives were hired just to throw everybody else off. Your father wanted the Mican inheritance to go to you, his only blood heir.

"What was with the post-its?" asked Charles, his interest showing despite his intent.

"The professor wanted to save Helena's soul. He had done his early anthropology studies on the Indians of Peru. We all know that they believe that a photo takes the soul away. Professor had his superstitions."

"Whose to say he wasn't right," said Helena.

"Fortunately, the professor was an obsessed record keeper. I found his secret hideaway and . . .

"Where is it!" shouted Charles.

"No way, client o-mine. I'm not that stupid. You see, Charles, I found out all about you during this investigation. You are not a Mican at all, are you? Daddy didn't even bother to adopt you. But he did make one stipulation is his will. If Helena did not show up alive before your twenty-third birthday, all Mican properties would go to you. He had no other blood heirs."

"When did investigators start investigating their clients? I think you should end your little story now," said Charles.

"As a last wish, just let me finish. I'll hurry. Helena, I'm sorry, but the Professor is dead. It was a natural death. He died quickly and thinking of you at the end."

Helena stood with her back against the fireplace, her arms pulled tightly behind her. A look of amazement and grief shot at Charles.

"You! my own bother. Betrayer!" she screamed.

"Ah, sister, almighty sister," Charles laughed, "you were always father's love. I loved you too. Until I found out he wasn't my father. I actually grieved for you when you went missing. I was totally bereft. And then one night while eavesdropping at the study door I heard *Father* talking to his attorney, going over the whole story. I hated you and him from that moment. Mother went crazy, crazy as a goddamned loon. Left me alone."

The movement came so swiftly that I jumped out of the chair. A cobalt streak hurled at Charles. Charles screamed "no, no Helena, stop!" Then the blood spurted from his right arm and Helena pushed him against the wall, her big hand around his throat.

"Get the rope in the corner. Tie him up, fast!" she yelled.

We tied Charles up so well that even Houdini would have had a hard time escaping. Prince had wandered in doe-eyed and still drugged, but his deep growl told me he would rip Charles's throat out if Helena told him to.

"I still don't understand it all," said Helena.

"It was all for money, pride and you should understand this, inheritance. Charles felt left out of everything. Your mother wasn't the only one that went loopie."

"She's not my mother."

"You were supposed to appear just before Charles's twenty-third birthday. They had both hidden you away, come up with the phony story about your birth. Professor figured, with your studies, he could convince you of that."

"It was very cruel."

"Yes. Very cruel. Anyway, two things foiled the plan: Charles hired me and, I'm real sorry, your father died."

"Somehow, I knew father was dead," she said. "Please, continue, Ms Boone."

"What really brought it all to a boil was that ad I put in the paper. "

"What ad?"

"I wanted someone to contact me about you." I told her about the ad and how it probably freaked Professor Simpson when he read it in the Roanoke paper. "When I traced your possible whereabouts to the college, the professor lost his cool. He was old, tired, too. So he just, well . . . I guess couldn't take the stress anymore."

I suppose we let out anxiety and frustration and pain in many ways. I think Helena probably hadn't felt too many emotions in years, until I told her about the ad and she burst out laughing. Spasms of laughter.

"Did anyone ever answer the ad?" she asked.

"You bet. I called into my answering machine a couple of days ago. I think I got about twenty calls. Ads may not be an investigator's best tool. The world is too full of needy people."

We left Prince to watch Charles until the police could come for him. Helena walked out of her home holding my hand.

"I suppose your wondering if the world has changed much," I said as we came to the barbed wire fence.

"Yes, that and what am I going to do with my life."

"Well. First, the world hasn't changed much at all in the last ten years. There's evil and good and it's sometimes hard to tell who is and who isn't. There's lots more fast food joints, more television, more computers, and we're still pretty much a democracy, even if our streets aren't that safe. Second, *you* can do whatever you want. I think you're about to become a millionaire and then some."

We headed into the setting sun and I put all the windows down so that the evening air could wash out the stench of the past.

"I'm practically an orphan now, Miss Boone," said Helena.

"It's not that bad of a life," I said. " Sometimes families can do you in quicker than anything or anyone else. Being alone is not always a bad thing."

The missed clue is something investigators have to get used to. It's a sinking feeling, a draining of the blood from the vessels of your brain, the tightening chest, the voice that calls to you *stupid shit, pay attention from now on!* I had never told Helena my last name. And then I again felt the gun on my neck and thought that I needed to find a new line of work as soon as I got home.

"All passion is not for money only. I love Charles. I want to be with him. We arranged it and you're not going to ruin it," Helena hissed.

"Was Prince in on it, too?" I asked.

"Very funny. Now there's a road a half a mile down, after the curve and on the left. Turn in there and go until I tell you to stop."

"That's why you didn't just kill Charles when you had the chance."

"Everything worth having is worth waiting for, planning for."

"When did you contact Charles? He was only twelve when you disappeared."

"I waited until he was of legal age, when else."

"You and Charles will never get away with this."

As I rounded the curve, I could see two police cars blocking the way. Old Betty had been paying attention. I pressed on the gas, waited until I'd gone up to fifty and jammed on the brakes. Helena went headfirst into the windshield, the gun popping out of her hands and into my lap. I grabbed it, jumped out of the car and stupidly flung it toward the police. I suppose I was lucky they didn't shoot me.

Well, that was my first and last case. My lawyer friend, after more scotch, laughingly suggested I stick to infidelity cases. I couldn't think of anything more depressing and dangerous for a single orphan. So, I took a job in the County Public Library, and now I spend my time looking for lost and rare books. As Mr. Sartre said, "Everything's back to normal," and I've never been happier.

II

LIVES AND REGRETS

It is too late! A funeral train comes gliding by your bed, in which Passion and Feeling assume bodily shape, and things of the mind become dim spectres to the eye.

Nathaniel Hawthorne
Twice-Told Tales

DAUGHTER

The baby fat seeps out of her as she leans over the yellow gladiolas. Only a mother can measure every pore, count every cell that conspires to drain the life from her child. My daughter slips away from me before my very eyes. She does not die from disease, she tells me, but from unrequited love. It is a process that I watch, but cannot stop, that fills me completely with loathing for the perpetrator, that takes my breath away. I see her hand move to the buttered flower as though her arm has no will, then the growth is torn from the earth.

I never liked him, from the beginning to the end of my setting eyes on him. Too tall, too slim, too dark, too handsome, and somewhat driven. I called him lithe, like a young girl; not yet a man. But when I look back on him, I will make myself be truthful. I know it was true love, as true as any can be, truer than I had ever had. Aaron. He had to have such a name. The rod. I remember that snake, that biblical anomaly that made me immediately hostile towards him. Too many begats.

"Why must you gauge everyone I bring home, Mother?" she had laughed the words. "It's like you're measuring how much air they have in their bodies. You want to pop them up, don't you?"

We did the mother-daughter dance around the kitchen, slicing tomatoes, peeling potatoes, all nostrils flared, breaths coming fast. We jostled each other, moving this way and that, from sink to refrigerator, while the aroma of garlic and onions and basil and thyme pranced around the thick air. The shrill music of her times, not mine, assaulted me like chanting without praise.

"Where have all the litanies gone?" I asked.

"Oh, Mother the Obscure, what the hell is that supposed to mean?"

She ate well while I watched, as she had since babyhood, often going for three servings, a child consuming life.

And so this morning I find her rocking back and forth, arms pinioned around her legs, pink toes dangling over the side of the chenille spread, going to market. White puffs sprout from between her toes. She is wailing softly, an incessant plea o love, o love, o love like the low moan of a dying loon or a French horn in need of tuning. A single sunray swims through the window and lights her hair to golden sheen. I imagine a halo there. Until he came into her life, I had not hated for a very long time.

LANA

As the red orb shimmered through a sharp orange blade that cut the sky in half, and purple tongues licked at the ashes of the world, Gaston Boudreaux looked west, measured the distance from the setting sun to the horizon, swallowed loneliness, clucked his tongue and yelled *veins! veins!* The cattle flicked their ears, turned slowly and marched towards him. He squinted through burning eyes. Sharp marsh wind blew clouds of hayseed into his face. He waved his big hand at the wind as though the act would clear the air, bring rain, batten down the dry earth.

Gaston was an impressive man; tall, bulky, barrel-chested, raw breath that smelled of onions, powerful leathery hands, muscled legs, and hair that had recently and irrevocably, changed to stark white. His eyes were blue like the stolen crystals from King Louis's crown. They linked him to his French ancestors who had escaped persecution and settled in south Louisiana. But Gaston knew little of the history that flowed through his loins, nor would he have cared should he be so informed. His heart was broken, the fissure widening with each day of the last three years since his wife Lana's death. She had been his breath each morning. It seemed that he no longer possessed the necessary experience that would help repair his heart. His religion was of little use to him. The Catholic Church had lost his soul thirty years ago when Father Martin had refused to baptize his twin girls, dead when his wife Lana had delivered them into his hands. The church did not honor innocence and for that he remained a man with no anchor. His sons were abducted by another war just last year. They had been his future. Now, he coveted his land with a weakness that poured liquid grief into his lungs. He had once believed himself a simple man; love your family, take care of the land and life would follow. "I am an old man," he said to the wind, "waiting for death. My thoughts fly out of me like *tee-gris* from the persimmon tree."

He let out a long breath, called *vien* again and listened for the expected low moan of his cattle. The sound came like puffs on the breeze, hungry and beseeching. The land was dry and dying. There had been no rain for two months and the drainage from the bayou was now but a trickle. He already knew there would be no rice harvest this year and not enough money to pay for seeds and fertilizer for spring planting. But he would pay the Negro family down the road, one of the few farm working families left in the parish. In the old days they were *locataire,* their pay was just letting them live on the land. This family, the Guidrys, owned their land, but the tan, mixed children were going their own way. Only one boy was left. The father was long dead in a hunting accident, the mother, they say, is crazy. But Thomas had helped him, worked harder than most grown men. Gaston could see him walking away from the shack, his mother standing on the porch, kicked up dust and rocks jumping at his feet.

He turned toward the approaching cattle, their moans throaty and frightened, three black figures moving at him, silhouettes swaying against the fading light that was slowly overtaking the world, whispers calling forth dusk. A Brahma, a milk cow, and her calf. Gaston had sold the rest of his herd last June; better they went to feed the troops. He had thought of his sons the night he had made that decision. He remembered the country sounds enveloping the night and his heart had hurt. He had hoped, but could not pray, that his dead cattle would become his sons' rations. He had sold twenty-five heads for half of what they were worth. "Eat my sons, eat and come home," were his last words before sleep had finally come to him and he had lived another dreamless, hollow night.

Impatient, the young calf pulled on his mother's teats, then banged against the udder with its head. Gaston knew that the calf was hungry, that the mother had given all she had for a while, that all three were weary of eating brittle grass. At least Gaston would be saved the chore of milking. "Suck *bebette,*" he whispered. "Suck until you burst. Let nature take her course." The Brahma jiggled his head this way and that, ears popping against the gray wrinkled leather of his scalp, flies dispersing and returning like gathering atoms. The rocking hump on the Brahma's back reminded Gaston of a tumor that should be sliced away, like a rotten breast. Shoes, thought Gaston, you will be shoes one day, after you have spent your seeds. The milk cow was called Betty at one time. Lana had named the cow on the day it was born six years ago. He would not speak the name now that Lana was gone.

The cow nudged him from behind, a gentle touch. Evenings made Gaston sad now. A feeling he had experienced briefly when he was growing up; when his sister drowned off Pointe Jude while netting for drum fish; and the time Papa had to shoot his horse. He had been sad then and now and everyday since Lana had died of the cancer. Nothing took the dull ache away. It just came rolling into him, over and over again. *C'est Malade,* the old people had called this feeling.

What was the land without her? His two sons off to war somewhere in France and the Pacific, the last he had word from them. That was months ago. He tried not to think of Abert and Marcel dead. How he loved them. Tears wet his cheeks and he wiped them with his hand, staring at the moisture as though it were blood. His hands, so hard and brown, black spots sprinkled around his wrist. Sometimes he saw blood oozing from scabby places, but he was always careful not to let Charlotte see. Why do you keep your hands in your pocket all the time, *Granpere*? She had asked him when she came to clean the house. *Depeche*, he told her. *Depeche.*

The three figures stared at him, their brown eyes reflecting his image, they waited for his guidance. *Un, deux, tois,* he counted, pushing his hands into his pockets. *Vien.* The three heads bobbed, hesitated, then sauntered toward the barnyard, passing Gaston slowly so that he held his hand over their backs and delicately felt their warm bodies move under his touch. *Master, master,* they seemed to say through their puffing noses. Lana, Abert and Marcel flowed through him and he gasped. The three animals would stop at the barn entrance where they would patiently wait like children anticipating the ministrations of a father at the end of a full day.

To the right of the barn, a triangle in the sky, was Lana's house. She had wanted it built like a perfect square with a dunce hat, one large window in the attic that overlooked the eastern pasture. There, she had said, she could do her sewing alone and watch the sun rise over their land. She had taken the picture from one of those fancy ladies magazines his sister Ida brought over all the time. Who made square houses, he had asked her. But he had done the best he could, measured and sawed and measured again. And on three sides of the house he had built porches that reached from one corner to the next and twelve feet outward so that rocking chairs and butter churns and children could find a place overlooking the fields. "*La, la,*" she had laughed when she described what she wanted. "Like the pictures. *C'est bon.*" This will calm me, she had told him, make our future spread out before us. A place for the babies to play. How he had loved her laughter floating in the air, her perfume like old roses, her breasts and stomach growing and pushing against that green dress. Thank heaven she had not seen her sons go off to war. The red wild roses still clung to the posts of the porches, and all this summer, despite the burning drought, they sprouted and made flowers as big as his hands. Their fragrance filled the air day and night, so that he had no peace. But he had carried buckets of manure to them so that they would not only grow, but thrive. Gaston could not fathom why he longed for the pain that the roses brought to him.

And inside this house, propped up against her side of the bed, was his rifle. Always used for killing only for food; ducks and quail and deer. He remembered suddenly the little bear he had killed out near Bernard's marsh. To this day he was sorry for that, although he was only ten and Papa had said the meat was the best in young animals. Tender, not like old animals with stretched and used muscles. He hadn't known the laws of nature yet. The rifle. He pushed the thought of it away for later and walked toward the waiting cows. He pulled his arms behind him, fingers intertwined, his head bowed, a man wanting.

Had Abert and Marcel killed other men? It was a question he had tried to ignore, but now it came like a flash when he saw the dead hen hanging upside down on the fence. He had wrung her neck that morning, watched her flail around the pen, then collapse. He had cut her head off with Abert's little red hatchet. What would his sons be like when they returned? Yes, they will return. But they surely have killed other men. What choice would they have? What could a father do to ease such memory for them? Deer and chickens and cows to the slaughter pen. And snakes, moccasins in the rice fields, my life for theirs. The one that had bit Papa, when he had pulled out his knife and sliced open his own leg. No grimacing in pain, no sound, right through the two red dots, and him saying Gaston, *regarde fils,* do it fast and it don't hurt you too much. He shook his head as though the action would push the thoughts away. I am going crazy. *Malade.*

Shades of darkness had come. The three animals waited. Gaston filled the old buckets with corn and salt, poured water into the trough and walked away from their begging breath. He could feel their eyes on his back, almost hear their thoughts: shall you forsake us, too? He walked quickly toward the house knowing it was too soon for him to go inside. Darkness was not yet complete. But he had at least moved away from condemning eyes.

He sat on Lana's rocker, the one her father had made when Abert was born. It still smelled of pine and baby flesh. His land was now shrouded by a deep blue blanket, flat on all sides, and the ducks had flown toward the waters, replaced by nesting black birds that made the pecan trees look full, like fat ghosts. Rows of dried corn lingered against the cobalt sky, and a delicate breeze massaged the rice, making a low hushing sound that inflated both time and space. Loneliness was so intense that Gaston decided at that moment that he would plant no more crops until Abert and Marcel returned. And if they didn't, well that would be the end of it.

The bills had piled up. He had no courage to pay them. He rocked. Charlotte would do this for him in the morning. Lotte, his grand baby already sixteen, collecting donations for the Red Cross. Such a wonder this child of Marcel. He wanted to leave her much of the land, for it was Lotte who cared for him now, who made his days just a little more bearable. What had Lana called her? Yes, little twinkle.

But what would this land be worth to Lotte? What if the war continued on for years? There would be nothing left. He would not sell to that company that sent that young man here three times already. No, I do not sell! No, no, no. My sons, my sons must give permission, he had told them. Then he had found out from Henry that it was not the land they cared for, but the oil and gas that lay underneath. He could see the future. The marshes flowing away to the Gulf, land turning gray, leaving dead fish and scurrying crabs and stinking frogs. And out came the tides until there would be nothing left. "Mark it," Papa had yelled when they had pulled in the nets weighed down with crab and croakers and trash fish. "This is life. This is what God meant for us to be like. Stay here and all will be well." Yes, Papa.

"Yes, Papa," said Gaston and realized that he was talking to his dead Papa and making a long crown of clover, twisting and tying, so that time had passed and he could not remember how he had come to the porch. Darkness wrapped around the house. Again, he had lost all sense of time and place. This was happening more often, and he became afraid. " But I will not sign, ever," he said, teeth clenched so hard his jaw ached. "Texas Oil Company be damned, the war be damned. God be damned."

He was hungry. Lotte had left him a plate of fried chicken and rice in the oven. He would eat his own rice from the plant in New Iberia. How long had it been since he'd cut his own rice, rode the combines, the dust from the wheels rising into his face so that he had a hard time breathing for weeks afterward. And still today he had problems with his lungs. No matter, a farmer can't smell the sweetness of it all if he doesn't do the work himself. The plate was cold, the food hard and dry. He ate the rice with a spoon, tasting Lotte's good gravy. But the chicken sickened him; he called *menew, menew* to the barn cats and threw the chicken out onto the grass. They fought, the black mother cat winning, and ran under the house.

He thought to let Lotte know not to cook for him. He would do for himself with milk and crackers and vegetables. He found that he could no longer eat meat. He wanted to talk to Lotte, really needed her at that moment, for he felt himself melting away again. Melting ever since Lana had died, faster and faster when his sons were called away. Enough of this sorrow, he told himself. Enough. Lana would be sad if she knew how I am about to give up. He forced himself to think about the business of the farm.

He wished he had listened to Lotte and allowed a telephone. He could call Harlin Battien, tell him to come and cut the pastures to the east, mow hay, feed the cattle, plow, start the winter fertilizers! He had made a good business, that young man Harlin. Lucky that he was refused by the army, something about not hearing guns. Harlin had taken over care of almost ten farms already and owned the largest caretaker company for the drafted men in St. Martin's Parish. Gaston had listened to Mr. Roosevelt and understood the dangers coming from the Germans and especially the Japs, understood that war must be fought again, that it would be a long time before anything would be the same. No, it would never be the same. Yes, tomorrow he would tell Lotte to get him a telephone.

His bed was cold every night, even in the heat of summer. Clean white sheets no longer welcomed him. The idea of sleep only made him lonely, for he knew he would wake up. He always woke up. "What is memory?" he asked, his voice like a mist in the darkness. He knew his way so well, he often forgot to use the lights at night, except when he longed for news of his sons. But not tonight. He didn't want anything. Especially not the dreams that came to him at night, like the time Papa's whole herd got into the bitterweed pasture. He had left the gate open after picking two watermelons for the picnic. Mama had asked him. "Deux, Gaston" she had laughed, holding up two fingers. Mama with her hands talking. The cows' bellies had grown fat and they mooed and cried for days and the milk was no good. Papa said they lost money. Didn't Gaston know that farming was like a war? "No, Papa, I'm sorry, I didn't mean to."

Tears were on his face. He cried too much lately. His head fell onto Lana's pillow, his eyes closed and he knew that this was where he wanted to die.

The morning came swiftly, warm and bright and noisy with life. Gaston had slept through the night.

"*Granpère,* I saw the chicken bones under the steps," said Lotte accusingly. "I know you didn't eat again. You will get sick." Her pinkness and the words rushed into the kitchen before Gaston had coffee. His mind was still fuzzy from sleep and no dreams.

"Lotte, it was late. I wasn't hungry. Come give me a hug,"

"Now I bring stew. Will you eat that at least?

"Yes, yes," he smiled and kissed her on the cheek. Lotte looked so much like his family. Clean, bright blue eyes that almost had no pupils they were so light. "Don't clean today."

"But I must, "she laughed and moved toward him, embracing him. "Sit, *Granpère,* I have something for you. A letter. I picked up the mail for you, so you wouldn't have to walk so far. You forgot to look, didn't you?"

"No, I didn't forget, Lotte."

She pushed him gently away from her, looking up into his face. "Don't be afraid. Those letters come in different envelopes. They bring them to us. This one is in *noncle* Abert's hand."

"You read it to me."

Lotte sat at the kitchen table and pried open the envelope that looked like it had been opened and resealed many times. She waited for Gaston to sit across from her, his arms on the table, hands clasped together, his eyes already wet. "*Eh bien,* read," he whispered.

May 12, 1944

Dear Papa:

I write to you fast because our unit will be sent out very soon. I cannot tell you where or when, but there will be an attack. I'm sure you already know about many already.

Know that I am alive and that I love you. I know that Lotte is reading this to you, so I tell her now how much her uncle loves her and to take care of you, please. Take heart.

Papa, I will come home soon. God will not allow Hitler to continue. I see you walking our fields in my mind and I walk with you right now. Put your hands behind your back like you always do and think of me walking towards you.

With all my love, your son, Abert.

(Papa, I have heard nothing about Marcel. So that is good news, yes?)

"I think he is in Italy. Roosevelt says Italy will fall soon. *Noncle* Abert's eating spaghetti already, *Granpère,* with a beautiful young girl on his lap."

"No. Lotte, we have not gone so far yet. The news is not good yet."

"And my father, where is he, then? You know so much."

"He is in the east. The islands, I imagine. Poor Marcel didn't even know where that was when he found out where he was going. The war goes better for us there, I think. The Japanese attacked us like cowards."

"Why didn't Abert ever marry?"

"Why do you ask that now?"

"Oh, just curious. Alice Hulin at the bank had a thing for him."

" A thing? He does not fall in love yet."

"He never will. He should have been a priest," laughed Lotte.

"No," said Gaston, standing up and shuffling toward the kitchen door, an old man, his chest burning. "No priests in this house. I must go to the chickens. They need feeding."

"I'll see you tomorrow then, *Granpère.* Eat, or I'll tell Mom on you. You know how mean she can be." She opened the screen door before him, a light touch of her lips on his chin, and ran down the dirt path to her old black Buick. He did not watch her leave, but looked toward the smoking fields. Henry Terrier was burning sugar cane for the winter. The smell filled the air with sweetness. Lotte's old car crackled away down the graveled driveway, chickens and ducks scattering from the assault of the great engine, wings beating the air. Fear rose in Gaston's stomach.

The egg snakes had been at the nests again. Brown shells littered the ground, crushed and pasted yellow against the hay. A pile of manure was evidence of the raid. One long indentation swiped through the middle of the dark green pile. The smell was wholesome, earthy, of *merde,* yolks, hay and reptilian consumption. This was the bayou smell, rich and sharp. Gaston saw that the hens had sat down again, retrenching and laying for a second day. Their squawks were throaty, subdued, and they looked at him accusingly. Why didn't you protect our treasure, the yellow eyes spit at him. You, you, where were you? He reached under his oldest hen, Henrietta, and found a salvaged egg, still warm, and he imagined it pulsating. He put it back.

Gaston filled the tin plates with crushed corn, clucked his tongue and counted his hens. Twelve left after the raccoons had visited last month. They had killed the mother hen. "Eat, little ones," he said and walked across the barnyard to a low-hanging pen. The enclosure was fashioned with the oak trees he and Abert and Marcel had cut down on the west pasture some twenty years ago. The boys were still so young, but they chopped and chopped until the trees fell to the ground. They had felt such pride with that accomplishment. Lana had made their favorite banana ice cream. He had turned the handle of the ice cream maker, tasted the rock salt, and scraped the paddle for Abert, the chunks of banana clinging to the spoon as he feed his child. It had been one of the best days of his life. The moma pig grunted and banged her head against the fence. She had given birth last spring. The babies were so big now. These he had decided not to sell, but to save them for Abert and Marcel. Pigs would be a good market when the war was over. Pork would bring big prices, he was sure. These animals would give his sons a new start. Gaston threw a bucket of cabbage, carrots and corn cobs into the pen, then opened the gate and put a block of red salt in the trough. Ten pigs, two mothers, one father and babies. Yes, a good start for a pig farm. Cheaper than cattle to run and less disease. Doctor Maisel had been drafted, so no veterinarian was available. He would be careful with these animals and eat only chicken.

The sugar smoke thickened. The east wind pushed the burned fragrance to him, like the arsenic he put out for the barn rats. Horatio had died of arsenic poisoning before Papa could tell what was happening. How he had loved that horse, the tapping memory of him that came to him now. Tap, tap, tap, remember me. And Madame Blanche, reading Shakespeare to her class before lunch and the boys' return to work. They only went to school in the morning then. Yes, he remembered, Shakespeare was why he had named that white horse Horatio. Horse eyes black as night. Madame was small and yellow with skin like paper, gray hair pulled tight in a bun. How she had loved Shakespeare.

"*Petites,*" her voice shook with her head, a deep unexpected voice that came from little red watermelon lips. "you are to make friends with Monsieur William Shakespeare. You will memorize his words. They will be lights for your life. *Eh bein.*" She had popped the little brown ruler against her black skirt as she talked: pop, Gaston, pop, recite, pop, Hamlet's, pop, speech, pop . . . The low moan of the milk cow vibrated in the air. Gaston looked past the shadows that moved across the gray and peeling gate. "Not in the stars, but ourselves," he whispered. The pain was dull, coming from far away.

"Gaston! Eat your eggs before you go outside, you hear me boy. *Depeche tois!*" "*Au, ma mere.*" The chickens are running out of the house, screeching at the moon, hurry, run, run run the sky is tumbling down, the snake is coming and smashing our babies, the spongy embryos sucked into the belly of the black twisted whip. "But the snake must live too," Lana said, "All things must live. Abert, Marcel, stop, do not kill that snake, it eats the rats. We do not need the arsenic." But she is dead, was all Gaston could know as he leaned against the fence, his mind moving away from him, pain running down his left arm until all life turned to black.

Gaston had built his home for his new bride in the summer of 1920. He had been lucky to come home from the war. He had seen so much, the world's *malade*, and a miracle had saved him from even being wounded. He had prayed then, every morning and night and into times when it wasn't even possible to tell which was which. He had lost his mother's rosary. He had been so careful with it, wrapping it in the little black handkerchief she had given him and stuffed it in his right boot. The raw bleeding of his feet, the rotting boots from the putrid water. He had pulled his boots off in agony and now the rosary lay somewhere on the battleground of France. He had found French compatriots, their language similar but rough. The prickle from his raw, wool uniform had been almost unbearable, lice and fleas and other insects he had never seen before. So small he couldn't see them, just feel the infernal itching. They got into the feces because there was nothing to use for wiping, not even leaves. Hands always smelly, wiped on the dirt, fingers in his eyes to push away the burning mustard gas. His bayonet stuck in the stomach of the young soldier, blond hair matted by dirt and blood, blue eyes like his, begging for mercy that would not come.

Gaston Boudreaux had come home, but not his brother Raymond. And Papa was still alive, tall and dark and strong. The Negro boys from down the road came to work on the farm. God knows they needed the money. Their daddy died at Verdun and they didn't even know where France was; and their mama made spells with the cross so that the parish priest said the devil got in her. But, his house was built square, divided into four rooms; a bedroom, a kitchen and a bathroom and, Lana had insisted, a dining room for Christmas and Easter. She had expected a big family. He had surprised her on their wedding night with a big, white bathtub held up by legs and feet like a lion. "Big enough for many babies!" she had laughed. That night they bathed together, something he had pushed away from his mind while they were courting. But now they were married and making love in a bathtub was not a sin anymore. He had been a young man who had not needed the pleasures of flesh and perfume and grunt. But Lana had come to him riding in a black buggy, a brown-haired girl, clean and innocent, five feet tall, with small white hands. Her father was bringing corn and she had decided to come with him. He was seventeen; she was fourteen. A year later, war had come. He had come home, worked the farm and finally believed himself worthy of her. They married. She had waited for him all those years.

It has been so long, Lana. She wanted a red front door so she could tell everyone where she lived. "Just go to the house with the red door." Her laughter tinkled through his body and to his chest that no longer felt pain. A red door and a memory still covered by rings of smoke. He must tell Henry not to burn too far to the ground. Let the winter grass come up. Through the haze a bright flash startled the air and a white egret rose up smooth as the Holy Spirit, turned in flight towards the low marshes, westward, where it had been born somewhere at the beginning of the world. Gaston knew he had grown old and that the sun had vanished to the other side of the world, replaced by another mist the color of corn tassels. He was seventy years old and in all the years from his first to last memory he had seen nothing like this come from the black Louisiana soil. He turned away from the image, fear and longing overtaking him, and walked through the red door and sat at the head of the dining room table, his place as husband and father. A long white tablecloth lay over the dark wood, all ironed and bare. At the other end of the table sat Madame Blanche, her hands resting on the table, so translucent that Gaston could hardly distinguish them from the table. She smiled at him and spoke in a strong voice, smoke pouring slowly from her mouth : "*Eh bein,* Gaston, so this is how you intend to die? The gun in the closet? To sin and not be resting with Lana in holy ground. What did Monsieur Shakespeare say, Gaston? You did not learn your lesson?" And then she was gone.

"Mr. Boudreaux. Mr. Boudreaux. Can you hear me?" Gaston heard the far away voice of Captain Smythe, and beyond his name the booming of guns. The war is over he thought, I came home. I know I am home. "Mr. Boudreaux. It's Doctor Bryant. You're at the hospital. Do you hear me?"

Gaston opened his eyes and saw a young man leaning over him. His face quivered and smiled, then a hand brushed his forehead. "*Granpère*. It's me, Lotte. You'll be fine."

"Lotte," he said. "How did I get here?"

"I found you when I went to bring your supper. In the barnyard. The pigs were out and pulling on your pants," she laughed. "If it weren't for their grunting, I may not have found you for a while. They sure love you."

"You've had a heart attack, Mr. Boudreaux," said the young man. "A mild one. But a heart attack just the same. You need to take it easy."

"I want to go home," Gaston whispered. "Now."

"No, *Granpère*. You must stay for a few days. Then we'll take you home. Right doctor?"

"As long as someone will stay with him for a while. Keep him calm. No strenuous work. I'll check you later," he said, pulling the sheet over Gaston's shoulder, smiling at Lotte and leaving the room.

"Cute, huh, *Granpère*?" asked Lotte, her cheeks flushed.

"You like him, no?"

"Yes."

"Lotte, what date is it?"

"July 1."

"Year?"

"Why, *Granpère*, it's nineteen forty-four."

"What news about the war?"

"There is the great battle in France. General Eisenhower is there. They say we are winning. Mr. Roosevelt is confident."

"Yes. He always looks on the bright side of life," said Gaston, turning his head toward the window and the beam of light flitting through gold spiraling dust. "Any more letters?"

"Yes. Moma got one from daddy. He is in the Pacific. You knew that already. He too is alive. He says he loves us and will be home soon. They always say that, don't they? That they'll be home. Anyway, he wrote to tell you something. Oh, and Mom says she'll come to see you soon."

"What does your daddy write me?"

"He writes: tell papa to save the pigs."

Gaston found that he was laughing. And Lotte laughed with him, throwing her arms around his chest, her hair tickling his face and smelling of lilacs. Not at all like Lana.

"Marcel could always make me laugh," he said.

"I must go now, I'll be back tomorrow. Rest." She kissed him on the forehead and vanished from the room, in a hurry to meet life head on.

Gaston went home from the hospital a day earlier than the doctor recommended. But he had insisted and Lotte had given in. Doctor Bryant had promised Lotte that he would look in on Gaston and he would pick her up so she could show him the way. "Ah, Lotte," Gaston had smiled, "you are one for the record books."

On the stove was a pot of chicken stew, still warm and smelling as fulfilling as life itself. White rice was heaped in the blue chipped bowl, a spoon sticking into the mound ready for his supper. He filled a plate with rice and scooped a ladle full of stew on the rice, a chicken leg plopping onto the mixture. Gaston sat at the kitchen table, alone in the falling dusk, and ate his supper while he watched his friend Henry bring the cattle into the barnyard. The echoes of the grunting pigs danced in the night air and he went to the hall closet for a sweater. That he felt cold in July was a fleeting thought, so entranced was Gaston with his own energy, his need to walk outside and smell his farm. Abundance surrounded him. He felt it in his bones. Not even the Depression had touched his family deeply. There had always been enough food. The fresh and clean air of the country had cut the early mornings like a knife and in autumn and in winter the blade sharpened to slice the black earth and push nurturing refuse down deep for the spring. And he had shared with his neighbors, those who had less than he had. Lana had said that was what God wanted, the sharing. That was life, like new cats hissing in the cane fields, snakes moving over the levees, seeking cool water in the rice channels. Gaston moved his head right then left, his vision softening the horizon. He listened with all of his strength, taking in the thousand sounds cracking over his land and he knew that he would hear this very moment in his sleep and he would finally be able to dream. And he heard Lana call him: "Gaston, come, it's ready, *depeche tois, depeche tois*."

That night, Gaston listened to President Roosevelt on the radio. The humming of the airwaves was magic. How did that happen, the sound racing through the air all the way from Washington to his farm in Louisiana? Why didn't the birds and rain stop the voice of this President, the music, the bands playing, the stories that made their way to him? "We are in the final stages. . ." said Roosevelt, talking about the landing on the coast of France. Many died, but the allies had been successful. Time was running out for the Germans. More than two million troops the man said after the chat was finished. How could two million men land on a far away place? How could one of those men be Abert? Somewhere in a place called Normandy, a place where people spoke the language he spoke. Good, he smiled, Abert can practice two languages. Maybe there he will have a girl on his knee like Lotte had said. Maybe when Abert got to Paris he would write that he was coming home. Surely the war would be over then. The announcer named Gabriel said he was signing off for music. A man started to sing. The swing, Lotte had told him one day, and she had danced around the kitchen table, her green polka dot skirt swishing until she was finally out of breath. Gaston turned the sound down and went to his bedroom. For the first time in a very long time he turned on the light.

Lana's clothes still hung in the closet and the scent of roses clung to the fabric and the shoes and every nail and board that held the things that had touched her life. Gaston ran his hand over her good dress, a dark blue silk dress with white flecks, like bright stars in the night. He pulled the dress to his face, burying his nose and mouth, breathing in and out and finally releasing sobs that wracked his body. He tried to call her name, but the sobs were overpowering, wrenching and finally painful. Fear stopped him, fear of death, of another heart attack. Rest, the doctor had said. He pushed Lana's clothes away from the wall and looked at his rifle, imagined the bullet blowing the snake's head away, the black and pink piece of life flipping high in the air and floating down into the water. He let the clothes fall back over the gun, closed the closet, turned the light off and went back to the kitchen to listen to the music.

November 3, 1944

My dearest Papa:

I know that you have not heard from me for a very long time. Whoever gets this letter first, my dear wife Mary or you, please rush to tell each other that I am alive and am coming home. I can tell you now because the news is all over the world by now. I was with MacArthur at Leyte in the Philippines and am proud to tell you that I served my country in restoring that country to its people. I was wounded and have been in Australia for some time. I cannot for sure tell you when I come home, but I will.

You see, Papa, I lost my leg during the battle, so I suppose I will have to be pushed around from now on.

I did not write that to Mary. I don't know how because I'm afraid she will not want me anymore. Please, Papa, you tell her for me. Then when I get home she'll be prepared to see me. I don't think I could live with the look she would give me seeing me and not knowing before. Thank you, Papa.

They tell us that the war in Europe may be over soon. Abert may be home before me. I go to sleep thinking of our lives there Papa, even though I will not come home a whole man. I depend on you to help, like you always have. Remember the day I fell out of the hayloft and broke my leg. How you worried over me. It is that leg that is gone.

I will close for now. The nurses here are mean as hell when we don't listen to them. I am supposed to be resting. What else can I do with no leg, huh Papa?

Your loving son, Marcel.

Mary did not take the news well. She retreated to her room and would not talk to Gaston for a week. Lotte cried for her father, then went to the Red Cross office in town for advice. Doctor Bryant was consulted also, and Gaston hired Thomas to build lifts and ramps at Marcel's house and the farm so that Marcel could get around in his new wheel chair. And Gaston visited his friend Henry for the first time in a year. Henry's yellow retriever had puppies and Gaston wanted two; one for Abert and one for Marcel. He brought the puppies to the farm, not four weeks old, and placed them on the red and blue plaid blankets from his sons' beds. He brought them his old shoes and a clock and rubbed them when they whimpered for their mother. By April the dogs were running through the fields, their heads pushing against the wind, their red tongues bouncing against their cheeks. And Gaston knew that dogs could smile. Just look at them, he told Lotte, like children full of life. On the twelfth President Roosevelt died, and for Gaston a part of his life came to an end. On that same day the American army marched toward Berlin. He knew then that Abert was coming home soon.

Spring was a bright time for the Boudreaux family. Marcel had arrived home, still loved by his wife despite his infirmity, admired by a daughter who would forever think her father a hero, and cherished by a father. The family had heard from Abert, who did not perish on French soil, but had been with Eisenhower when American soldiers had walked into Dachau. "My days shall be haunted forever," he had written. The day after he had received Abert's letter, Gaston took Lana's clothes to the young couple down the road. Thomas had married and his wife looked just Lana's size.

The Boudreaux land reaches to the marshes in the west, and it was there that Gaston rode out in the early morning, the old horse pumping, determined to hold her rider through the embankments, her large eyes drifting down, her radar attuned to the slithering enemy. Egrets turned their heads and looked at him with suspicion, then they sprung upward, white wings extended, floating away from the invader. Wild geese abandoned their nests, hiding in the cattails and willow overhangs, knowing that the interloper would soon leave. And water bugs bobbed and scurried, amassed throughout the clean, primeval waters. Gaston took in this life, breathed deeply, then flung his rifle out as far as he could, watched it plop into the water, hover in disquietude and then sink. Perhaps, he prayed, the tide will pull it out into the gulf to sink into the muddy waters.

IDA MAE

My name is Ida Mae Pugh. I turned sixty just yesterday. It's morning, real early and the sun is just pushing up beyond the scrub. I like to sit on my porch in the bright morning and watch the jays hop from bush to bush, pecking at every berry and bug. They flutter against the pink sky like black finger puppets. Time will be they'll all be gone.

Hot, strong coffee sends the punch through me. Some people say it gives them the jitters, so they stop drinking it. Most fear cancer. That's not a fact for me. So, here I am sitting in my usual spot, rocking chair easing into the horizon. I'm supposed to be thanking the Lord for a new day. But this is what I'm really thinking. That just about the time you cross one river, life turns into a piece of dog poop.

When I woke up this morning, I heard that bunch of yellow Ts singing in the china ball tree in my backyard. Some folks call it a chinaberry tree. We used to cut a bamboo stick and spit those shiny green balls at our play enemies. Didn't need guns to have fun. The Ts make a sound like *blureep, blureep,* and I wish I could touch one live one, just once. I'd hold it tenderly in my hand, touch its yellow bill to my old mouth and know the mystery of life. I believe it'll whisper to me. My mouth has lines, and makeup and lipstick only makes it look worse, like that lady in a play I once saw on PBS. I even sent them twenty dollars, it being worth my time not to watch those damn commercials. The show was called *The Mad Lady of Shylow*, or something like that. She drank tea and said that Paris was lost. She wasn't crazy either. Truth be told is I feel like her sometimes. Ts are not Ts, like china balls are not china balls. The people at the Audubon Society call them yellow-billed cuckoos, *coccyzus americanus*. Latin, hot diggedy, I know Latin. I learned new names of birds I'd seen and heard all my life. That's enough. I ain't joining no tree society. They're a nice bunch of folks. Poor Ts, though, I'm always picking up their eggs from the ground. Seems they have a hard time building good nests. That's by their nature. I used to put the eggs back in the nests for them. But, James Toret, the President, tells me not to do that 'cause the mothers will just leave the nest. I like them, I sure do. They eat those nasty orange and black fury worms that can strip an azalea bush in one night.

I got lots of Ts and azaleas in my yard. Many yellow birds and vermilion azaleas. *Vermilion*. I love to say that word. If I could paint a picture, I would make everything *vermilion* and green.

Well, what have I got to do with myself now is the question. A beautiful spring day like this smelling clean, and me just ready to head off and nowhere to go. For more than forty years I had something to look forward to. I had a job at the Orange Crescent Rubber Company, with all kinds of benefits like health insurance and even some retirement money. Pretty good considering my only education is one year of secretary classes at the trade school. I put up with that god-awful smell of burning rubber all them years. Reminded me of that incense they use at the Catholic Church, the one the Mexicans go to. Only time I was there was to see Jamie Gonzalez put to rest. Nice man. Left five little kids the night he was robbed and murdered for just thirty-eight dollars. They wouldn't have him at my work, so he went right ahead and started his own business. He did a fine job with my yard. That smell was unforgiveness to me. But I got used to it and stayed skinny 'cause I just couldn't eat there. Ate in the morning and when I got home at night.

I always walked to work. I loved the sweetness of morning, the wet grass with little spider homes and inky caps sprouting along the sidewalk. They'd kill a body if you ate 'em. I would start at one end of town, just about here at my porch and go straight through town, past Olsen's Department Store. When I was little, I used to buy a whole bag of candy corn there for just one nickel. Back in eighty-nine, I watched the dying of all the cottonwood and jacaranda trees along Main Street. They say it was the cold winter, but I saw the dark smoggy clouds coming in from the east. I wore white gloves when we went shopping downtown. Moma did, too. We were ladies back then. I figure I walked three miles up and three back. Six miles a day going at a good pace. I sure been ahead of today's healthy advisors. I enjoyed that forty-five minute stroll through the Florida mornings, just cool in the winter, and if it rained, well, an umbrella did just fine. Besides, rain is an afternoon thing here. It begins with lightening sizzling in the air so bad it smells like sulfur brewing in the lakes.

I love the mornings best. The sun glows, the world I know comes alive. My daddy made us kids get up before sunrise. "Up and at 'em, mother earth is waking up. Least you can do is join her!" he yelled. I miss my Daddy. He was the only man I ever loved. Sometimes I feel all left behind. Now what will morning be? I had friends at The Crescent. Friends to meet at the First Baptist Church, to have Christmas and Thanksgiving with, someone to talk to and just to smile at me. We expected it was a lifetime thing. Maybe I should think about leaving here, since I got no real cause to stay. But where would I go? There's the fear part of my life.

I'll specially miss Shirleene. Her wild red hair streaked with gray, puffing around that pretty face. She has the prettiest blue eyes. I just never knew anyone else whose eyes sparkled. Not like mine that are dull brown. My eyelids droop now and I can hardly see sometimes. Shirleene says I can get that fixed easy. Me and Shirleene worked together at the Crescent for twenty years. She's only forty now. I 'member her first day; laughing young thing. I fell in love. She has her job and I don't and I wonder if we'll still be friends. We think that things like this, situations, won't change how we are with each other. But they do. We just go from one thing to another, but it shouldn't be that way with people, hopping from place to place.

Nobody explained about our future when they let us go. I guess they'd say why should they, it ain't their problem anymore. Social Security is still far away. I cain't get Medicare yet. I'm by myself. Never married, never been lonely. Just my niece Laural that lives in a trailer out near Zolfo Springs. Heck, she couldn't help if she wanted, not with them little kids screaming all over the place. Always wiping their snot noses on their sleeves no matter how much Kleenex I given 'em. At least they don't visit here much. I cain't take 'em. Lucky I have a society meeting next Tuesday night. That's something to look forward to. I can still afford to bring something for the potluck supper. They all like my cornbread and chicken wing stew.

Yesterday I found some nasty condoms in my front yard. Rubbers they're called. Rubber supplied by the Orange Crescent. I once asked T.J. Smythe, owner of the Crescent, about that. If the company made them things. He laughed at me. "Damn Ida Mae," he said, "I guess you really never had it." He walked away laughing at me and I was a joke all around the office for about a week. I never heard such stupid jokes. I'm not offended by sex jokes, just real dumb ones. And I sure didn't like the way T.J. told everyone about my question. Made me a bit put out and feeling like I'd missed part of my life.

The last couple years at The Crescent was real hard for me and my friends. But seems like we'd all get up and go to work anyway if we had our jobs back. Our lives back. We got no representation here, specially not in Florida. Never heard of a union situation around here, not in all my life. T.J. blamed his misfortunes on the environment people. Said they were the ones making him spend all his money. That's when he cut our pay by three dollars. Six months later he took away our life insurance. People at the society told me it ain't true what T.J. said. There's just not a big market for his rubber anymore. Anyway, he polluted the Osceola River, him and his other cronies. It's a dead river now. I used to swim and fish in that river. And I found a dead T under my kumquat tree. I stretched my old liver-spotted hand under the mulch and pulled it out. That was two weeks ago. It was an omen and I said so at work. The next week they let all twenty us go.

Omens are God's hints to us mortals. I know that is true. All my life I've lived with omens; summer nights without black cicadas screeching in the oak trees, a spider web without a spider, or people with two color eyes. Last year the rain burned our skin. I read the papers, don't get me wrong. I'm not at all stupid like T.J. said. Acid rain is what we used to call it.

I suppose I need to stop dwelling on my problems. Work things out. I cain't say I didn't know it was coming. I put my application in at the Wal-Mart. They sent fliers around the day before we were let go, like they knew what was gonna happen. They're making a super store with groceries and just about anything a person could need. I think I'd make a good associate. Could be better than at The Crescent.

The Lord says turn away from bad thoughts and I do.

The Edgewater Village for retired persons built a senior center last month. I saw in the paper that anyone over fifty-five could join the activities. I had thought about going to some place like that when I retired. But, well, not anymore. This old house of mine is leaking. Been here since I was born. Guess I'll die here. Nice little two-story stucco bungalow is the way real estate people would call it. I used to keep chickens in the backyard until the code enforcers came around. Said I couldn't keep farm animals in the city limits no matter how much taxes I paid. First time I put up an argument to city officials. Now I just plant tomatoes, peppers and squash. All that chicken droppings of the past keep them growing real good. Those ten poplars Daddy put in years ago must be twenty feet high now. They sway back and forth in the wind like they was dancing. Yellow and green heads back and forth to a symphony. Violins and flutes are my favorites.

I signed up for a tennis lesson, if you can believe that. I got pretty strong legs with all the walking and strong arms from moving boxes around when lifters called out. I always admired tennis players. There's more dedication there than any other sport on television, specially the old players. Followed Billie Jean for years. I started watching it all the time when I got cable a few years ago. Now I need to cancel that. Maybe. It sure cost a lot. But I'm still gonna go to tennis, no matter what. I cain't die without that dream coming true. I even bought a can of yellow balls on special for a dollar ninety-eight at the Dollar Store. When I go to bed at night, I close my eyes tight as I can. Before I fall to sleep, I watch the ball fly up, up, and I swing my old wooden racket. It's like a red stripe zipping across the sun. The yellow bird flies over the net far, far away from here.

I've been waiting for my tennis partner for more than ten minutes. She's not late. I'm early. None of my friends play tennis, actually they don't play anything and I couldn't get one of them to start. So I asked for a partner when I signed up at the Center. I checked a while ago, just to get the name of my partner, as I was here before her. I wanted to conjure up an image I could work with while I waited. What does she look like, what would we look like playing, what would she say when she finds out that I practice on a brick wall in my driveway? I read the list on a green book that looked like the accountant's at work. It said 9 am- H. Stone and I.M. Pugh. Helen, Harriet, Hannah, Hope.

I got my hair cut yesterday afternoon at Margaret's Hair Styles. She works out of her house in the bedroom of her son Darren. He was killed in Dessert Storm. One of the first. Marge says she can feel him, so that's why she set up her business there. He was a handsome boy. The gray hasn't crowned me yet, as Shirleene used to say about her own head. Mama was stark white by the time she was forty. Died standing at the kitchen sink humming a tune. I was sitting at the kitchen table when she crumbled to the floor. Mama's gone ten years now. Daddy's been gone twenty-five. We used to walk to work together on mornings like this. Ashes to earth.

I count six courts. They're all busy right now. I'm supposed to play in ten minutes. I've tried not to look at my watch too often, so I won't look anxious. Court four is where I'll begin. Two other women are there slapping the ball back and forth and hardly even missing. Pretty and slim, with leg muscles popping in and out as they run back and forth. Mine are just as good, I know that much. All of a sudden tears are moving down my face, and I wipe them away quickly before somcone sees me. I'm afraid. I rub my racket up and down with my right hand and grip the handle just like Billie Jean showed us in that film I borrowed from the library. Thumb position, hold the racket at your side, look at your. . ..Don't cry, Ida Mae. Don't cry.

"Hi, are you Ms. Pugh?" I look up into the blurry face of a man. The sun is in my eyes so I blink and hold my hand up.

"Yes, I'm Ida Mae Pugh," I say. He moves to my right and away from the sun. I can see him full now, the hand reaching out, big and clean, crinkled black hair like a bush on a bed of dry leaves. A gold bracelet slides down and falls around the middle of the hand. Gold sparks reflect from the sun and shoot into the air. I reach out, careful to show that I am strong, that I can hold my own. I grab his hand, too tightly, I know, and pump up and down, too many times, I know. I look into his eyes and see for the first time since Daddy, kindness in the eyes of a man.

"It looks like our court is still occupied," he says. His voice is low, almost a whisper, and it rumbles instead of talks. He is smiling. He is dark and clean shaved. His smile opens his mouth to white, straight teeth, and then wrinkles look like they're cutting into his cheeks and go from his eyes to his hairline. He has black hair with streaks of gray. He is a handsome man, I think, and I am ashamed for looking.

"Do you still want to play with me?" I ask, looking down at my white sneakers, PF Flyers from Wal-Mart. $9.98 on sale. I look at his shoes. They are Nike, white, with a dark blue check mark. "I can come back another time," I say.

"Why would you want to?" he asks. "I don't mind waiting a little while longer. Are you in a hurry?"

"No," I say. "I have all the time of my life left."

"May I sit with you then?" he asks.

"Yes, you may."

He sits to my left, his tennis racket resting on his knees. I read the name on the handle, but do not recognize what it is. He smells like gardenias and sweat and warmth.

"How long have you played tennis?" he asks.

"Not very long," I say and add: "Actually, I only practiced by myself for a time. So, I cain't play much, really. . ."

"Well, I guess we'll be in the same league then," he says.

"Thank you," I whisper.

"Oh, they're leaving. Let's have at it, Ida Mae." He places his hand on my elbow, so I stand and walk toward court four.

He goes on in front of me. His head is turned toward the court so that I can see the side of his face. He is a man with character, I decide, because he does not look mad at the world. I hesitate so I can measure him. He is wearing a baby blue shirt, white shorts, and white socks that go all the way up to his knees. *Ida Mae, you forgot your manners.* I mouth the words so that no one will hear me. I do not know his name. Harry, Howard, Herman . . . Mr. Stone. I turn toward the closest side of the court, deciding that I will take the sun in my eyes to start. He turns, looks at me and points his racket toward the other side. "Ida Mae, you start on the other side first. I have sunglasses. God knows who built courts to take the morning sun."

I say nothing, nod my head and quickly walk to the far court. I position myself (as Billie Jean says) to the right of the court, near the white line. I hold my racket out correctly. I feel perspiration under my arms. He is standing across from me and to the left, bouncing the yellow ball, head down like he is thinking how did he get himself into playing with such a woman. I realize I left my can of balls on the bench I was sitting on. I look at the bench and see they have rolled to the ground.

"Let's just hit the ball back and forth," he yells, "until we both get the hang of this game."

I nod again and wait for the yellow T to fly at me. I watch him throw the ball to the ground and swing at it. It goes up into the air and over the net, plopping about four feet in front of me. I walk forward, turn and hit the ball too hard. It flies straight at him and he lifts his racket in front of his face. I think I hear a *thwat* when the ball hits the racket and bounces up and hits Mr. Stone's side of the net. I look at him and he is laughing, slapping his knee with his left hand, racket on the ground.

"I'm very sorry," I shout. "I told you I wasn't real good."

"Yes. I see that, and I'm just a little worse than you!" He laughs.

We both get the hang of hitting the ball after a while. Suddenly the sun vanishes and a hot wind pushes against me. I smell the rain long before it falls. Sand whirls in little tornadoes on the side of the court and they make their way across the court to Mr. Stone's side. The tall palm trees look like ladies caught in a wind cloud, their green and brown arms waving madly.

He is walking towards me and I imagine he is jogging in slow motion. His smile is like a black ink mark across his face. "How about we go into the club house and get a glass of juice? Maybe this weather disturbance will pass us up," he says.

I nod, knowing I did that too many times already instead of talking. He must think I'm stupid. He takes my elbow in his hand and I let him take me to wherever he is going.

I am surrounded by voices and laughter. We are sitting near a large window that looks out at a golf course. Dark clouds hang over the world, the wind is batting trees and bushes every which way. I don't remember getting here. I turn my head and look around the room. It is full of people, mostly women in white clothes, white and red hair, and red lips. I smell coffee and eggs and bacon and feel a hole in my stomach. I am hungry. Mr. Stone is sitting across the table from me and it's like I can feel his eyes, like a cat hiding in a bush. I am out of place, out of time and I am the mad lady. At any time, they will look at me, see my shoes, my hair and my unpolished fingernails. I squeeze my eyes, afraid I will begin to cry.

"Ida Mae," he says, "please don't feel like you have to stay here if you don't want to. It's just that, well, I just moved here last week and I don't know anyone yet." I look at his face and know that I was right about his eyes. He is staring at me, like he wants me to say something, make it all right.

"I'll stay. But I never been here before. I don't want you to be ashamed about that," I say as soft as I can so no one else can hear me.

"Why would anyone be ashamed of you? You're a lovely lady. And I would say, Ida Mae, quite a brave one too."

"I'm just trying to live good, Mr. Stone. There's nothing brave about that," I say.

"My name is Homer. So let's start by being friends, you and I. There's no bravery in that. I think you'll be very easy to like."

"Welcome to Carlson, Florida, Homer Stone," I say, lifting my glass of water in a toast and not caring what anybody thinks of me now.

"Thank you," he says.

I feel something coming behind me. Like the one eyed cat, I see things coming my way.

"Well, Homer Stone, have you moved in, my dear?" peeps a woman's voice. She is beautiful. Tall and blond and tan skinned. I look at her mouth and see no lipstick hiding in wrinkles, no dark spots or out of place hair on her chin. A long arm reaches for Homer, pink fingernails and blue veins slither past my face, then her body folds over him and she kisses his cheek.

I want to run, to disappear just like when I was at The Crescent and they laughed at my questions. I slide my chair away from the table and wait for the right moment to leave, my feet placed to push, the napkin back on the table.

"I'm just fine, Eleanor. I've moved everything in and your friends were so kind to arrange my things in my apartment. But, let me introduce you to a friend of mine. Eleanor, I'd like you to meet Ida Mae Pugh, my tennis partner." He is standing, his arm stretched toward me. I don't know if I should stand or hold out my hand.

"I'm so glad to meet you," she says. She does not offer her hand to me. I look at her straight in the face, at narrowed eyes, and pursed lips. I see the lines now, the half-closed eyes, the looking down at me thing. She reminds me of Jenny, Shirleene's Siamese cat. Scratch you anytime for no reason. Persnickety is what.

I am not happy sitting here listening to them talking about things I don't care about. I want to go home and take a hot bath, sit on my porch and listen to the Ts again. I will walk tonight is my plan. Instead of morning, I will change to evening walking and start from my house, go through town and turn around at Harper's Quik Pick at the corner of Spruce. I might even buy myself a Mary Jane for the walk back. Yes, I will turn my day around.

I don't know where the last hour or so has gone. I know I ate eggs and bacon, and that's just all it was. I say thank you to Homer and he asks me to come back.

I have made up my mind. "I want to play tennis more," I say. "On Tuesday is good, for just one hour. 'Cause I have things I want to do besides, lots of things and you're welcome to come, too, sometimes," I say. The words are pouring from somewhere in me and I don't know from where.

"I'd like that," he says. "What other things do you do, Ida Mae?"

He is not making fun of me, I know that, even though those words would make somebody else think so. "I have a society meeting on Tuesday night. Audubon. You're sure welcome to come."

"I will. Tonight?" he asks.

"Yes." I say.

"Should I pick you up?"

"No, I like to walk. It's at the town library every other Tuesday night. Five-thirty. And we have pot luck suppers. I like to walk," I say. "By myself."

THE MANOR HOUSE MUSICIANS

Manor House was the ugliest building in St. Claire, Louisiana. It was constructed the year after the Great War, funded by leftover Louisiana Progressives who believed that the state had an obligation to provide for the sick, lame and mentally ill men who had survived service to their country. The building reminded its early inhabitants of military barracks. When the edifice was pasted back together with the red bricks so distinctive of Roosevelt's WPA, critics referred to the monstrosity as the precursor of VA hospitals. Indeed, WPA workers had carved the bold-faced relief (called *mezzo-rilievo* by an out of work architect) above the entrance to the building on instruction from the head of the work crew who had grown up in a Chicago orphanage called Manor House. So, thanks to the New Deal, or not, the building remained not only standing but also open for service for over seventy years. The old generators hardly needed to warm a brick structure in the humid hell of south Louisiana. Air-conditioning was not even an issue. Window fans had been screwed haphazardly into the windows of the dank rooms that housed the patients. Green mold decorated the inner walls, and closets and variegated nooks and crannies echoed hoary and undisturbed homes of spiders, rats, and roaches as big as a grown man's thumb. The scuffling sounds of the creatures filled the night, forever stinking the air with ancient urine.

The dispossessed entered Manor House at a dramatic rate in the eighties; most came to stay, for they had no choice. Few willingly called the place home. Additional rooms were slapped on to the original structure in nineteen seventy-one, for America had begun to age. When, in nineteen eighty-three, Washington demanded death statistics in exchange for federal funding, the first report placed the death rate of Manor House residents at eighty-five percent. The real figure was ninety-nine. The patients that did leave Manor House alive left only to die at the local hospital. Statistics, upon which funding was to be based for the next fifteen years, were calculated by an orderly named Wayne Houdin. Every year, Wayne turned in the number *85%,* no matter the arithmetic gymnastics necessary to arrive at the bottom line. There were no great oaks with dripping moss surrounding Manor House. The hoots of owls and songs of doves came from far away, for the grounds within three miles of the building had been leveled. The great and majestic oaks had been used to build tract homes as the town of St. Claire grew to a population of 4,563 by nineteen eighty-nine. Ten years later, Manor House still beckoned, filling all who entered with profound sadness. Their lives no longer stretched out before them.

The *St. Claire Times,* the town's only newspaper, had written some ten editorials during the past two years, urging the city, state or federal government to do something about not only the unsightly nature of the structure, but the dismal conditions of its inhabitants. Nothing had been done. Manor House was a nursing home, a rest home, a rehabilitation facility, called whatever would allow it's continued existence for skimming money from government pockets. An investigation conducted by the FBI showed that the Bileau family of New Orleans had purchased Manor House in nineteen sixty as a convenient place to send the many family members who were incorrigibles, as Hattie Bileau once described them, or who the family believed had "deserved" a place to rest before dying. One historian, a young man working on his doctorate in history at Tulane University, had estimated that over one hundred Bileaus had resided, and died, at Manor House. He intimated connections to the Mafia, but never published his research, failed to pass his oral and written examinations, and was never heard from again.

One year ago, nineteen ninety-eight, Manor House was sold to a large corporation, an event that was remembered by some citizens of St. Claire because it was spring, when the people of Louisiana look forward to green fields, jumping croakers, drumfish nibbling on the oil rigs, and crawfish rapidly treading their way to the levees that cordoned off the sections of green waves of rice, their spiny legs uttering escape. The *Times* chronicled the sale, noting that much money had changed hands in the halls of the state legislature in Baton Rouge. It seemed as though the editor finally gave up his crusade, if editorials could be called such a glorious human endeavor. The paper went on to more mundane subjects, announcing the first crawfish boil of the season, to take place on Main Street on Saturday, April the eighteenth. The whole town was invited, as usual, and there was a call for anyone who could entertain the town with "good old-fashioned music."

Jason Albright had lived at Manor House, in room 206, for six months, as a result of a motorcycle accident on Horse Head Road on his way to a gig at a local joint called the White Eagle. It was frequented by both whites and blacks from the seamy side of New Orleans, gaining fame as a hang out for Hell's Angels types. Jason played the electric guitar for a group called *The Dreamers.* When the orange truck hit him from behind, its horn having tailed him for over a mile, Jason heard the crunch at the base of his back, but surprisingly, he felt no pain as he watched the earth hurtle towards him. At Manor House, he lay on a stretcher day and night. Only the clacking of the stretcher on the beveled wood floor offered him hope that he would one day be able to move something more than what went on above his shoulders. He told no one that he felt a fine-tuned tremor when the therapist buckled his hands to the cold steel encasement of the exercise bars. *Clackity, clackity, clack* was music to his ears, and with this sound he wrote music, tunes that stayed in his head like they never would before. He thought that the nerves below his neck had not died, but had simply jumped into his head. His memory and senses where now so extraordinary, so delicate, so far-reaching, that he could smell human longings, feel the approach of a fly from five feet away, taste decaying food on his tongue, see the fear in the hollow eyes of the other patients, and hear voices from behind doors.

And so it was on his return from therapy on Tuesday morning, when he was dividing his mind's energy between the clacking and voices, the smells of mildew, mold, shit and that stuff they feed the dying, that Jason heard the grand plan. He should have felt shivers down his spine, he thought, but that was no longer possible. He listened as the aide, Betty, pushed him against the wall near the administrator's office, straightened his covers, brushed the hair from his forehead, and then left for her lunch break.

"You all stay here," she said, reaching into the pocket of her white uniform and taking out a cigarette and a red and blue matchbox. She lit the cigarette, blew the smoke in Jason's face, coughed, then placed the cigarette in his mouth. He pulled in smoke until his lungs could hold no longer. The smoke burst from him and he smiled.

"You might try not spitting when you all do that," said Betty.

She turned from him, her round hips swaying, heading down the dark hallway and out of Manor House.

"Wait!" Jason shouted. "You could at least change my pee bag."

"Woo, wee, white boy. You be dead as a moccasin ain't for me. I'll be back in a half-hour or so. Bring you a bottle of Jax. You be good, hear. I put you in an interesting place, right entatainin. "

"You know I like Budweiser," he yelled. "Budweiser, Betty. Please?"

"Okay, son, I'll get you a Bud."

Jason liked Betty. She was the first black person that ever got close enough to him so he could know that it just didn't make any difference what color you were. He didn't consider himself prejudiced. Before the accident black and white was just something he never bothered about. Betty whispered in his ear that one day God would lift him up, promising to bring the great healer Reverend *Le* Roy (" not Leeeroy, " she had insisted) Jackson to see him, to put the Lord into him, make him rise up. And Betty had soft hands, big and black with pink palms that could turn him over with a gentleness he had never known; every day she washed his body, spreading grease that smelled of dead ducks on the sores that continually broke out on his ass. It was the sores that made him want to die, sometimes, that made him want to give up, to blot out the music and voices that grew louder every day.

Jason lay on his stretcher, the one strap secured across his belly, "so you won't fall and crack open all you working with for now," said Betty. He closed his eyes and thought of Nina, how she had always liked to take the top, how he had held on to his erection for her, and how her breath had stopped when she came. She had told him that it was his black hair and blue eyes that turned her on, the way he walked towards her, one foot placed exactly where the other had been, like a hungry tiger. When he thought of their lovemaking, he could feel nothing rise in him, not in his mind, heart or penis. It had *all* died. He thought he still loved Nina, but knew he would never see her again. Only his mother had come to visit him during the six months he had been at Manor House. All she did was cry, and ask sweet Jesus to help her poor baby. She had come three times and that was all. Jason saw that it was too painful for her to look at him, so he decided to forgive her. The guys in the band had sent flowers to the hospital, but not one showed up in person. He forgave them, too, and the drunk that had hit him. He had no strength for anger. He quickly trained himself to focus away from the past and onto harnessing his new sensual experiences, like the arguing coming from behind the door. The bottom part of the door was black wood, the top half-muted glass. Jason could not see movement, but he could tell that three people were talking. He recognized Boone, the asshole dictator who ordered everybody around, wouldn't even say hello to Betty when she said mornin' to him. He never trusted anyone who couldn't look another person in the eye. And then there was Nurse LeJeune; the shrillness of her voice was like a chain saw in his head. Jason did not know the third person. A man, a low, baritone voice, strong and mean, telling Boone and LeJeune how things were gonna be. Like he owned the place.

"Look, you two, Health International wants this place to make a profit within the next six months. That means we get rid of the parasites," said the man Jason decided to call Bruno.

"We can't just throw them out," shrieked Nurse Lejeune. "Where do we send them? Some have no families to go to!"

"Surely the state of Louisiana has those institutions still standing," grumbled Bruno.

"Yeah, yeah, they're still some around," whined Boone. "My uncle was sent to one back in the fifties. I remember my mother and grandpa drove me out to see him. Somewhere out in the woods. I still remember the smell of pine needles. And big daddy long legs crawling all over the place. It was winter. He died of pneumonia out there. Alone."

"Thanks for the memoir, Boone. But just find places. The accountants in Nashville gave me a list of the ones that have to go. They're costing us money. Get them out by the next month's audit. We don't want them showing up on the financial reports."

"But we can't just get them out so soon. It's the fourteenth. That gives my staff about two weeks. No! that's impossible," said LeJeune. Jason imagined her arms wrapped around her chest, her glasses falling to the edge of her nose.

"Two weeks," said Boone. "You heard Mr. Murphy. Here's the list."

There was silence, paper shuffling, a chair scraping on the rug, a click and then the smell of cigarette smoke, a just audible breath pushing out and then the blast of another breath sucking in.

"Oh, my God. It will kill some of these people to move!" hissed LeJeune. "I won't stand for it. I won't!"

"Shut up!" yelled Boone.

"Stop it, both of you," said Bruno. "There's twelve people on that list. Look at the figures next to each of their names. That's how much the corporation has lost in the last three months taking care of them. They can get Medicaid somewhere else. We don't do that anymore."

"Listen to the names," said LeJeune. "Theophile Hebert, he has senile dementia and served in two wars. Larry Harkins, an amputee with diabetes and a stroke. Jennifer Billings has progressive MS. Mrs. Landry. And Marie Nygen. She lost her children in Vietnam and then her husband was murdered for shrimp in Texas. She doesn't even know where she is. She flashes back and forth!"

"Then she needs a psychiatric hospital," said Bruno.

"They're aren't any for her. Remember, we send the mentally ill out in the streets to become homeless," said LeJeune. "And Jason Albright. He'll die of pneumonia, too. They won't even move him around out in the pines, Mr. Boone. It'll be just like your uncle." She started crying. Jason could hear the tinkling as the tears touched her cheek. Poor Nurse LeJeune, thought Jason.

"Just do it!" yelled Bruno. And the sound of the opening door hit Jason, the cool air from Boone's air-conditioned office patted his face, and he smelled men's after shave like sweat and shit and rotting flesh. Jason turned his head slowly and looked at Bruno. He was tall and skinny, his gray suit hung from him like the guy in the *Night of the Living Dead.* His hair was white, his face wrinkled and dry like fried chicken skin. Bruno looked at Jason, and when their eyes met, it was like when Jason saw his father's eyes coming at him, before he had picked him up and threw him against the kitchen wall, before he lit into Mama again and again and again.

Betty came back before her lunchtime was over. She was carrying a brown paper bag with two Budweisers and a box of colored straws. "I got you the one's that bend. It'll be easier for you to drink from, hon."

"Thanks, Betty. You're better than the best. I live for your touch."

"Go on with you, boy. I'm too fat and too old for the likes of you. Let's go to the garden for a while. Get you some sunshine."

"And beer, too," said Jason. "I got a lot of thinking to do."

"Too much thinking can hurt you. Makes you dissatisfied with what you cain't change."

"It ain't change I want, Betty. I need to stop that old train from running us down."

"What the hell you talking about?"

"Just get me to the garden, okay. Maybe I'll tell you later."

"Best laid, boy, best laid," said Betty, as she pushed the stretcher, the top of her body leaning over Jason's face, her big breast rubbing against his forehead, bringing comfort and a brief glance at what could have been. She hummed a tune that Jason knew well after these past six months. *Deliver us, Oh Jesus, from the hands of Satan.*

Jason had once watched a television program on gardens around the world. He had been high at the time, which was great because the colors were brighter than usual. Sometimes when he took a long pull, it was like that kaleidoscope kids played with. He imagined cool shade, chirping birds, the smell of his mama's gardenias. The garden at Manor House was hot and brown. Very few flowers spotted the ground, except for those considered weeds by most people. Dandelions and bitterweeds, sparse and gangly. Why was yellow the color of weeds? Betty pushed him in a circle, around a short fountain that didn't work. It had been white at one time, now fungus had turned it to steely green. When it rained, the fountain filled up, then the heat of the day cooked the water to green slim that in the evening became a perfect soup for mosquitoes bigger than horse flies. Betty had promised Jason to bring him out at night to watch the fireflies, but she went home at exactly five o'clock and didn't come back until seven the next morning. But old Theo obliged him and pushed him out every night about nine, guiding his stretcher slowly past the night orderlies, who simply saluted them and said "Ya'll be careful now, Mr. Bear. Ya'll be careful, sir." And so Jason learned that respect comes in many forms. Theo quickly brought Jason out of Manor House and through another dimension, introducing him to the heavens, the planets, the constellations, the Big Dipper, the Night Star, Sagittarius and Mars. And thus was opened the black hole that had become his heart.

Theophile Hebert, called "the Bear" by the orderlies, was the first friend Jason ever had over the age of seventy. Theo, as Jason liked to call him, was ninety-nine years old. Almost a century of life right in Manor House. He had served in both the First and Second World Wars and his stories were mesmerizing with exacting information; what people looked like, what they said, and even what time of day certain events took place. Theo talked about himself and his father as though they were the same person. Etteine Hebert had been present at the signing at Versailles. "Oh, not the Great War," Theo had said with widened eyes, his hands thrust upward, pausing for dramatic effect. "When Bismarck humbled France and all of Europe. The long march started then. That's when the sabers started to rattle, rattle, rattle through Europe." Jason could hear the clash of steel every time he heard the story. The staff at Manor House thought that Theo was in another world, so the world gave Theo an illness for what they did not understand. But, Theo knew how to survive at Manor House, because it was nothing compared to the horrors he had known. He was, above all, a generous man, recounting his travels around the world, how he had trained as a concert violinist, could play Cajun music on the fiddle and how he missed the buddies in his *fais-do-do* band, how he had reeled at seeing the dead at the concentration camps, grabbed Eisenhower's arm for support then heard the whispered song of the perished *for all time, for all time.* Jason had learned more from his friend Theo than anyone else he had ever known.

Betty jostled the stretcher and then it stopped near the only tree in the garden, a poplar that speared upward, so there was no shade except early in the morning and in the dusk of spreading shadows. Theo sat in a lawn chair at Jason's feet, his fiddle resting on his knees, his big hands almost covering the shiny brown instrument completely. The top part of Theo's body swayed left to right as he hummed, his head cocked upward toward the sky, eyes wide open to the sun.

"Theo, what ya singing, man?" asked Jason.

Theo smiled and his head slipped down until he was looking into Jason's eyes. "A story I used to play at the club in New Iberia. The French had many tales about life on the bayou. But every one of them is about how life is so short and how a man can get so low. I wonder why that is."

"'Cause they's Catholics. Damn depressing religion," said Betty.

"And you are, Madame?" laughed Theo.

"You know I'm Baptist. A high rollin' one."

"Yeah, but the food was heaven. More shrimp than a human could eat. That's how we got paid. Music for food."

"What's it called? Sing to me, Theo. I need to think. Sing in English. I don't know that French stuff," said Jason.

Theo shelved the fiddle under his chin, dipped his head and squished his chin on it. Then he closed his eyes, bit his lower lip and waited for the silence that only an old man playing a violin could hear. The sudden movement of his right arm was like a captured moth, fluttering and banging against a window. His leg started bouncing and the twanging sound of a fiddle crashed into his grinding, aged voice. The blast made Jason laugh; he had expected a sad song. He closed his eyes, remembering his electric guitar left in the lonely closet of room 206, and he cried so that his tears tumbled down the side of his head making hot pools in his ears.

Betty's salty, begging voice joined Theo's and they sang out, loud, unafraid, appealing: *I ain't dead yet, Oh Lord, I ain't. When ya come to get me, open the gate. I been so lonely, my heart is almost broke. I miss my sweet darlin' and that ain't no joke.*

A mosquito landed on Jason's forehead, the music stopped and laughter careened through the thick air. Jason opened his eyes as a balled hand wiped his forehead.

"How you doing today, Jason? I heard the music and just knew you and Theo were out here."

"Did you bring your flute?"

"No. It's hard, you know that. My lungs are turning to stone it seems."

Jennifer Bileau, née Billings, had been a resident of Manor House for almost two years. Her story was both ironic and sad, as though the gods had punished her for making the wrong decision. Jennifer had met Standiford Harrison Bileau at Tulane University three months before she was to take her medical boards. An invitation to a Mardi Gras ball at one of the elegant homes on St. Charles was supposed to give her a brief respite from her studies. She had sliced through every organ of her cadaver, whom she had named George, then had lovingly placed each organ in jars decorated with gold stars. And then Standiford appeared among the glitter and madness of New Orleans. Jennifer Billings from a South Dakota farm fell in love, was offered a life filled with money, a prominent name, and an immediate place in the world. At the blossoming age of twenty-seven, she married the only son of the owners of Manor House. Three years later, there was still no heir, and Jennifer found herself stumbling up and down steps, objects fell from her hands as though they had wills of their own, and the many doctors she visited could not tell her why she was losing control of her bodily functions. When she had to resort to using adult diapers, Jennifer plummeted into a deep depression. Her body deteriorated while she watched herself through a gilded mirror, the drooping eyelids one day, the sagging cheek the next. Permanence is a fleeting element of life, that is what she took to saying to herself, day and night. Her mantra. She took twenty-four pills a day, including Valium and scotch, for she had known early in the disease process that she exhibited all the symptoms of multiple sclerosis, for which there was no cure. The eminent Bileau physicians never told her the truth. But, it was the depression that sent her to Manor House, or at least the shame of it all. Thus, Jennifer became one of those well-deserved Bileau cases. For the first year, the family totally and unequivocally supported her. Unlike the more seasoned residents, she had a personal physician who saw her once a week, a hairdresser, a physical therapist and a psychiatrist. Standiford did not visit her, which was no great loss, since he had abandoned her even before the disease had diminished her. Jennifer was informed by the Manor House administrator, Mr. Thaddeus Boone, that her husband had divorced her, making her a ward of the great state of Louisiana, a Medicaid patient. Two months after this news, for which she felt liberation rather than remorse, Betty handed her a newspaper article torn from the society section of the *Times Picayune*. Next to the column that announced the wedding of Petrina Marks to Harold Stein was the article concerning the unprecedented annulment of the marriage of Jennifer Billings and Standiford Harrison Bileau. The Archdiocese of New Orleans had received word from Rome that underlying medical circumstances had given the act sanction. This was Jennifer's second moment of prominence, for her name would be forever affixed to a papal document. Hallelujah. The following month, her loving parents perished when their farmhouse went up in flames during a South Dakota blizzard. Jennifer's mind shut down. It was the only way she could commit suicide. She sat near comatose in her wheel chair. No doctor, nurse, aide or social worker could get her to react to life. Until Theophile Hebert came to Manor House, involuntarily admitted by his three daughters, and noted in his medical records to have senile dementia, be of unsound mind, incompetent, too old to have around.

Jason knew better, and so did most of the staff at Manor House. Jason had watched the change in Jennifer that Theo's music brought, what it did to Jennifer when Theo smoothed her hair back away from her forehead when she got all sweaty, how she felt life when he told her *life is life at whatever point we are in it, petit.* What did Jason know of it? He was twenty-five, paralyzed, bagged, gutted. He had taken a couple of college courses in psychology before dropping out. Applying that epidermal knowledge, Jason guessed that Theo was like a loving father, and he knew without doubt that music could save a soul.

The shadows were moving towards his stretcher. Jason could feel the air cooling down as a brief puff passed over his face. Theo had moved to hug Jennifer and the acid smell of old men burned Jason's eyes. Since the accident, he had realized that he was incapable of getting nauseous. He turned to the right, where he would look almost directly into Jennifer's crystal blue eyes. Her face was unlined, the tone of her white skin like porcelain, her lips lavender; a breakable, antique doll. Her body had shrunk since he'd met her, like it was dissolving or becoming part of the wheel chair. She would be a wheel chair with a head. Jennifer always wore black, in stark contrast to Theo's Hawaiian shirt; all lime green, golden yellow and bursting orange. Shocking pink flamingoes danced on the sleeves. Theo's eyes were deep blue, without the cataract film of the old. One fuzzy gray eyebrow streaked across his head like an undulating caterpillar. He was completely bald, his scalp dotted with brown liver spots, the under skin showing patches of red. He never wore a hat in the garden, no matter how long he stayed out. Theo's dark, leathery hand engulfed Jennifer's white, delicate hand. Jason had seen this bear

Theo help an orderly lift a dead patient from the floor to the bed, secure the straps tightly around the man, and say a prayer for his soul. To Jason, Theo was one of the bravest men he had ever met.

"It's going on snack time before too long," said Betty. "You want me to bring it out here for ya'll?"

"I'm not hungry, Betty," said Jennifer.

"I'll take hers and his," said Theo, pointing at Jason's stomach where the feeding tube dangled.

"I'll have my beer," said Jason.

Betty swung away toward the entrance to the building, popped the door open, and Jason heard the organ playing to a cascade of agonized voices singing *let me call you sweetheart.*

"Can you believe that shit?" asked Theo. "All the great music of the world, played in all the great gin joints of the world, for all of us that took care of this here world, for good or bad, and they insult us with that *merde*. I hope they fall down into a hole leading to hell."

"There are worse things gonna happen," said Jason. "I have to talk to you, both of you. You know how I can hear real good now. Well, I heard Boone and LeJeune and some big fucker talking about us. About twelve of us."

"Oh, dear God," said Jennifer. She pushed on the wheels of her chair with her balled hands until her face was almost touching Jason's. "How can anymore happen to us?"

"Just tell, Jay boy, and then we'll see what we can see, up in the tree, on bended knee, I often pee," sang Theo.

"Betty left me near Boone's office when she went to lunch. I heard Boone, LeJeune and a guy from the company that owns this place. They're gonna get rid of twelve of us here. That includes the three of us." Water streamed from Jason's eyes, but he felt nothing, not an emotion like fear or panic or loneliness, but tears of shear bone piercing weariness. How, he asked himself, could liquid make its way through his body, filter through his kidneys, rush to his eyes and he never knew what was happening. Paralyzed. What an unsubstantial life!

"EEH yah!" yelled Theo. "Them galdarned bastards finally figured out they ain't got shit business here in St. Claire. God, he has spoken."

"What do you mean? This is a tragedy. Where will we go?" asked Jennifer.

"Nowhere. We're not leaving this town. I ain't leaving this town. My daughters put me away, thought I'd die straight away. Horse shit to them is what I say, ten years of marriage they banged away, came running back to daddy and put him in harm's way, so I say good riddance and take the money, and show them the gate, Rachel, Rebecca and Raylene, I wish you never come back to see me in my bad old dreams."

"Nice song, Theo. But what the hell does it mean?" asked Jason.

"Means we gotta do something. Let somebody besides us know what's going down."

"Going down?" laughed Jason.

"The newspaper. We could go to the newspaper." Said Jennifer, sliding forward in her chair, her body twisting towards Theo.

"Careful, darlin'. Don't want you to fall. Cain't say many people around in town reads the paper anymore," said Theo.

"Not just here, all over. We could call the authorities," said Jennifer.

"No," said Jason. "From what I heard they're doing it all legal."

"Then let's go tell it up on a mountain." Betty stood near the fountain, her big hands on her hips, her feet glued to the cement walk.

"Betty? How long you been listening, girl?" laughed Theo.

"Long enough. If they let some here go, then they're gonna let some of us with jobs go. We need a plan. A plan."

A fiddle, a flute, a voice like God's angel, and a mind to write music became a miracle. From the night of April fourteenth to the early morning of the eighteenth, the Manor House Musicians practiced their song for the St. Claire town picnic. Jennifer had dictated a letter to Betty, who delivered the crudely spelled words to the *St. Claire Times* editor, volunteering the nursing home group. Quick to pick up a great story, the editor announced the group in his editorial, sprung for a half page ad, and went out to Manor House to interview the musicians. Harlin Boudreaux wrote an inspiring story, one that captured the imagination of the interns that watched the wires and Internet at all the major services in the world. Jason, Theo, Jennifer and Betty made both good copy and great photos. They were careful to give credit to the expert skills of people who worked at Manor House, which spoke to their humanness, despite the travails of their own lives. At first, no mention was made of Boone, Bruno or Health International. LeJeune was salvaged from disgrace, since good nurses were hard to find and she had a kind heart. There descended upon St. Claire such locusts as CNN, ABC, NBC and many others, all sending out investigative reporters to dig, dig, dig. Although nothing specifically illegal could be found, the news people made Boone and Bruno out to be callous creatures whose lives deserved little redemption. The Manor House Musicians were portrayed as people of great courage, whose lives had met with injustice compounded by injustice, so that there was no mercy except for the victims.

A large, white van arrived at Manor House at ten on the morning of the eighteenth. Betty had bathed Jason, dressing him in a clean white shirt, jeans, and cowboy boots her son Leonard had donated. Theo decorated the stretcher with red, white and blue streamers. Theo himself wore the gray suit in which he had come to Manor House, except that his left breast was now blazoned with twelve colorful medals, including a Purple Heart. In his left pocket, he told Jason, he carried a picture of Marie Carrone, his only true love, a nurse killed in Algiers. He had never liked DeGaulle, he said, as he walked towards the van. Jennifer did not wear black. Nurse LeJeune had bought her a present for the occasion: a soft yellow dress with a wide scooped collar that was trimmed with white lace. Jason saw the soft blush in Jennifer's cheeks, the moist eyes, and just a hint of a smile, as though she knew that this one day of her life would be worth it all. Betty went to the van last. She wore her navy blue dress, the one she saved for baptisms, weddings and funerals. An old red hat was securely Bobbie-pinned to her hair, for she knew that it was her job to bellow out the words to the song that would tell the world about Manor House. "Praise the Lord! Praise the Lord loudest as you ever have," Theo told her. "Follow the music, we'll be right behind you. I'll whisper the words if you get nervous," Jason said. "And me," said Jennifer, "my flute will guide you, softly, between words". "Yes, sir, sweet Jesus," Betty replied, "God sent me you like the wings of an angel. Us don't need to mind a wheel chair, a stretcher or no damn daughters that cain't take care of themselves."

The ride down the hill and to Main Street was interrupted only by flashing cameras. When the Musicians arrived, Jennifer and Jason were carried onto the stage by a delegation of admiring citizens. Betty and Theo walked up the stairs holding hands. The weather was hot and humid, but a last minute breeze eased the anticipation of the crowd and the nervousness of the Manor House Musicians. The Mayor spoke, congratulated the town for its community spirit, welcomed the news media and any other visitors. He was proud of his town, invited everyone to stay for barbecue, crawfish, catfish, beer and fireworks. Then he was silent. The air crackled with the voices from the telephone lines. Jason felt the tremors again.

"Courage," announced the Mayor, "true courage, that is, seems absent from our lives. For most of us, it takes courage to get up in the morning and go to work, to do the ordinary things that our holy men tell us are signposts of admirable and decent lives. And then we meet extraordinary people whose courage is not even imaginable to any of us. They tell us who we are, why we live, and what love is really all about. I will not say anymore, my fellow citizens. You know all about them, maybe more than you should." Holding his hands above his head, palms out, the Mayor signaled the crowd to hold their applause. "I introduce you to the Manor House Musicians"

Betty pulled Jason forward, unlatched the hinges of his stretcher then pushed him into a sitting position facing the crowd. She stood next to him, stiffened her spine and reached for his hand. Jennifer wheeled up next to Betty and took Betty's hand, her stiff fingers opening. Then Theo marched forward, clicked his heels and stood at attention next to Jennifer. His hand stroked her hair and he whispered words that only the four could hear. *What comes, comes. But ain't' we a sight and a memory.* St. Claire had never been so quiet. Not one crying baby could be heard, not a cough, or sniffle or giggle.

Jennifer let go of Betty's hand and took up her flute, placing it between her lips, then closed her eyes. It was the most peaceful sound heard down Main Street, St. Claire, Louisiana, U.S.A., ever. Piercing and ringing and floating, up to the trees the notes twirled and hung and fell on the heads of the crowd, as though anointing them. Those who would look close enough, saw Jason's lips move with each new note that came from the lady in the wheel chair. Then the treble softened, Theo put his violin under his chin and the music was like arrows through the clouds, up and down and around, like furies. The crowd stood with mouths open, then they swayed in unison, back and forth, side to side. Many began to cry, but their sobs were muted by the music. Then it stopped. Betty took two steps forward, folded her hands in front of her, looked upward and began to sing as the flute and violin created delicate waves of bliss behind her: *I am taken up with you. We are one, one in life. No man takes our lives away without leaving strife. They came from across the water, knee deep in sin. You are my brother, my sister mine. Take me up with you. I am not lost, people in life, where we die the good death. Shame comes to them, then you, but love shines through.*

Betty sang the words three times, each time in a higher and higher trilling tone. And then it all came to an abrupt end. After an eternity, the crowd let out a burst of air, simultaneous, painful, liberating.

The Musicians stayed for the picnic, and then they were driven back to Manor House. The next few days were filled with more interviews and photo opportunities. But they refused to sing again. The news coverage was so extensive, that an outraged nation demanded that Health International leave St. Claire. The company gratefully withdrew only when the town, which had sat on a rich oil field for many years, signed a contract with the company and purchased Manor House for a reasonable price. Manor House was refurbished, and the town sprang for a new garden filled with gardenias, camellias and azaleas. The town charter was revised, giving the residents of Manor House all necessary care within reasonable boundaries. Boone left town and was never heard from again. LeJeune was put in charge and allowed to hire a doctor to care for her patients. Theo got into the habit of visiting LeJeune every day. One night, as she worked late, Theo came to see her carrying the picture of Marie Carrone in his hand. Theo died in his sleep the following night, while he sat at his window watching wild geese fly across the full moon. He had turned one hundred years old the day before. Jennifer's MS went into bearable remission, so she played her flute every afternoon in the Gardens of Manor House, and spent one day each week giving lessons at St. Claire's middle school. Betty was promoted to manager of all non-nursing staff, continued to sing in her church choir and attend every holy event in town. She finally bought a new navy blue dress with matching hat when she turned fifty-five. Jason died the week after the grand performance of the Manor House Musicians. He had become dehydrated, an infection set into his bladder, then rapidly coursed its way through his bloodstream so that he became septic. Nothing could be done, the doctor had said, but they were amazed at the tremors that moved his body. Betty told them it just meant that God was bringing him over the threshold from a harsh present to a kind eternity.

The old fountain was removed from the garden and replaced with a statue of a young man holding a guitar. Years later, those who visited their loved ones at Manor House laughed because they thought it was a young Elvis Presley. But those who could look deeply into their souls would read and understand the words branded on the gold plaque. *Dedicated to a young man who listened to the voices and turned them into the music of life. Jason Albright, a favorite son of St. Claire, Louisiana.*

THE TRAIN TO PORT ARTHUR

It happened during a journey by train, on a dull August afternoon in 1955, just outside of Port Arthur, Texas. The ragged white boy stood cockeyed, a too big, dirty white undershirt falling from his shoulders, his left hand fisted and pushing down into his jeans, his head moving with the click-whir, click-whir of a robot, as though he were looking for an earthly target. His face was beautiful, crowned by long black, shiny hair, slicked upward and into a large curl that must have tickled his forehead. He was the boy from outer space, from Uranus, I thought. He smiled, then thrust his right hand up and out towards the train. I pushed my face forward, smashing my nose against the hot window, little puffs of steam marking the glass, my right hand ready for a happy reply. I hoped desperately, with all my heart, that he would see me, connect with me. *See me!* I whispered to him, willing him to hear me through the shimmering, curling heat rising up from the tracks. He looked straight at me and widened his smile. Then the boy lifted his arm high into the air, his middle finger jutting out from his clinched fist, teeth biting down on his lower lip, his mouth forming a hollow cave. The *you, you, you* jumped from the round pink orifice on his face, the sound jumbled with the blasting train whistle. *Fuck you!* he yells at me. At me.

It was an alien stab to my heart, a cutting moment, the epiphany that became a mere flash of memory, forever known as a demented and misguided rudder in my life. I lost my innocence to a young man whose anger at the world fell to me. A nonverbal instant. Children do not utter or act out the words that are meant to condemn, to belittle, to dismiss. But when their words are littered with those signs, their hearts grow cluttered, the meanies bump into each other as the thumps go on and on, and one white finger like a worm of hatred borrows deep. How trite it has all become.

Because Father worked for the railroad, his family was anointed as a class bearing the privilege of free transportation on the Sunset Limited. We could go anywhere in the United States, follow the rails for free. Of greater favor was that the privilege extended for our exclusive use of the Sitting Car. Mother saw in this gesture the sole value of our station in life, far above our singular and naturally discontinuous family. It was only in that rectangular and stuffy space that we were whole, absent the physical presence of Father, three ungrateful beneficiaries of his daily toil. In the end, his work kept his family at a necessary distance from him. This ever widening gap was almost all worth it, for the Sitting Car was our one great luxury. All other possessions came with the edifying words *scrimp* and *save*. How glorious to ride in the only car among the chain of rattling links that spoke of an inbred etiquette, a moving room fitted with a puffy melon green sofa and chairs covered with chocolate swirls of brown brocade. I imagined such pleasure to be much like the front rooms found in the homes of refined Southern families, as Mother called the houses on the other side of town. "Lordy, to live in such places would be just plain sinful. Jesus, it sure would be a pleasure," she said, as she squinted toward the horizon, wiping her greasy sweat with a rose embroidered handkerchief. When I grew to an age of pure reason, I knew those homes as only places, blue dots on a street map, empty caves hidden behind magnolias and azaleas, nothing more than places where money allowed the inhabitants to pretend. The arms of the chairs were inlaid with dark, cool cherry wood. And in the wood were nestled carved images of strange flowers and foreign grass. So I had just as much right to wonder as the stolid, marble flesh of gentility.

"Daddy, where did the Sitting Car chairs come from?" I had asked, hoping for a mysterious story.

"From Korea. Stuff from the Korean War. After we shot up their asses, we took what we wanted back," said Father.

"Is that from across the ocean?"

"You bet. And then they put it on the train in San Francisco. Just so you and your mother can loll around like little Shebas."

I passed time on our journey in a somnolent wonderment, tracing those engraved indentions with my forefinger, making a daydream about slant-eyed women more beautiful than me. The Sitting Car was carpeted and clean and deep green, so I was permitted to sit on the floor, my dress tucked under my buttocks, my legs folded to my right, patent leather buckled shoes with folded white socks borrowed from Easter Sundays. I was perched near Mother's feet, my body twisted so there was no way my privates could be seen. I had always received specific instructions from Mother, followed by warnings of frigid disapproval should I fail to abide by the decorum of young ladyhood. Mother's censure came swiftly in the form of a pursed mouth, piercing eyes, and the final pinch on my upper arm. I remember purple marks growing like an octopus on skinny, white flesh.

Mother always wore her navy blue dress on the train to Port Arthur. It had white polka dots that moved up and down on her bosom like stars twinkling on a dark sky. She was Cassiopeia in her big brown chair, boasting head turned to me. She who was to live forever, it seemed. The dress was her best home made yet, the rhinestone studded belt buckle acquired from Aunt Lila's leftover suit straight from high fashion New York. The buttonholes were primitive, for mother made all of our clothes on a foot pump sewing machine, and it was always the button holes that first announced to the world that our pretense did not extend beyond the Sitting Car. I saw clearly, feeling resentment rather than shame, the halting, slanting smiles of onlookers that said that the DuBois family was *less than* them. And there was Mother, standing straight and as tall as possible, a five feet tall little French lady descended from farmers in the Louisiana countryside, who spoke near to no English. In the fifties to use that language outside of the family or Church circles brought shame. Mother had a sixth grade education, and she spent most of her life atoning for that, using the Catholic Church as her rock. She early surrounded her children with a great wall of stoic duty, made with stone upon stone and unnamed sin upon unnamed sin; the mortar, the mix that held the edifice together had no component called charity. Mother's mouth was perpetually set in the particular edge of obligation, red lips, image left on a piece of toilet paper when she had finished her makeup, putting on her face, poofing. She smelled of the perfume from the cobalt blue bottle that was eternally poised on the top tier of her stone white dresser, the mirror reflecting the matching four poster bed.

I often watched her face as the train swayed to the rhythm of our times, speeding away from the screams in Money, Mississippi, where I was later to hear in hushed conversations of the murder of boy Till. Mother's dark eyes flipped through the passing world, never showing amusement. And I mused until the day she died about what really went on behind those black pools. She curled her coarse hair with Bobbie pins, hands moving like a humming bee, as though she were beset by furies until she pronounced her next move.

"Inez," she said, "get the box for our lunch. And go yourself in a hurry. Your brother is hongry."

The smell of rotten eggs bubbled up from the soil of southwestern Louisiana, and the hot air pushed into the Sitting Car, letting us know that we were nearing the town of Sulphur. My brother Theophile was stretched out on the sofa, languishing, threatening. This was his way of letting mother know that her insistence on his accompanying us to Port Arthur and to her younger brother's home interfered with his summer. Theophile, or Theo as we called him, was ten years older than me. He rarely felt Mother's demeanor, and in the last few months, he had ignored her rare attempts at exerting power over him. So he was allowed to be a layabout despite my protests. Mother said Theo had a place in this world, by his age, his manness, or by luck that he was his Father's son; these gave credence to his disdain for even her. He was heir to my Father. To my Father's what I cannot, even to this day, tell you. I did not like my brother. And that was at least confessional. I know I did not hate him. He was much like my Father, or at least I saw things that way. They were both my tormentors. Theo by his presence in my life, Father by his absence.

Father did not ride with us. He put us on the train and walked away before the train pulled out of the station. This was how he slipped away from us, bushy eyebrows, furrowed forehead, broad-backed Daddy walking away, never waving good-bye, only saying "take care now, ya hear" to Mother from the sidewalk. Not even a peck on the cheek. Was there shame in that act? He died the week after I turned eighteen and I hardly felt it.

The train stopped often, taking and leaving passengers, starting up as the wheels gnawed at the rails, like the grinding of my teeth when I am possessed by unwanted dreams. I often stood at the window during the trip, watching the flash of earth and sky slither back to where we had started. Stores lined the tracks like portents to lost enterprises of the rails and scattered poverty. Death bleated out in terror from stockyards, then oil and cornfields turned into silver and amber waves, while water towers defied gravity and we reached the edges of towns where church steeples declared that life was all planned, ordained, that we should move on quickly. Through it all, the rotten smell of sulphur guided the train, pushing it forward over the border and into Texas, where oil became the new air, pumped out of the earth from black fields of man-plants encrusted against the sky. My child's eye saw dinosaurs, raptured, ancient, threatening.

"Spread out the food on plates, *depeche* chil'. We're hongry. I tol' you two times now." She yelled, slit-eyed.

In the Sitting Car the air grew close and warm. Theo was draped like a snake along the sofa, his upper body hovering over the monopoly game we had played for the last hour. I had waited for him to buy Park Place. He always bought Park Place because he broke the rules, or made his own rules. To Theo, it didn't make any difference. He used his own monopoly "charm," a dark green plastic toy soldier, its helmet covering the face, a jutting chin, and a rifle aimed ready to the kill. Park Place, Broadway and the Reading were never within my grasp. I had long accepted that. I also accepted losing, and found stories of Monopoly games lasting for days one of the mysteries of life. But it was an early lesson in lowered expectations, in learning to live my mother's life.

"Come on, bird brain, move your shitty piece!" said Theo, swatting at me with his hand.

"I'm trying to figure where I'm going to land," I replied, counting the moves to Park Place in my head, the little silver dog clutched in my hand.

"You're such an ass."

"Theo DuBois, you stop your cussing this minute," said Mother, her voice singing.

"If you didn't make me come on this trip and play with this cry baby, then I wouldn't have to." He yelled, throwing the dice, rolling eight and moving the army man to Marvin Gardens. "See what you made me do, bird shit."

"Inez, get the lunch box out, ya here. Forget the game."

"But, momma, Theo's gonna move my piece when I'm gettin it," I whined.

"Stop that crying this very minute, Inez Marie, and do what I tol' you."

The lunch had been meticulously packed the night before the trip, for what good is ritual if it is not fine-tuned. Unlike our daily meals at home, the train ride offered choices: fried chicken, boiled egg, or baloney sandwich. My chore had been the careful wrapping of each piece of chicken, each egg, each sandwich in smoky wax paper, tape measured just exactly for security. I heard the cracking of the wax paper, smelled the chicken fried in old lard that was used over and over and saved in a Crisco can under the sink. The thought of the congealed, white paste topped by brown flecks of old bacon bits turned my stomach, bringing a sudden disorder to the journey. I peeled away the tape from one piece of chicken and handed it to Theo.

"Put a sandwich and an egg on the plate, too. You think I'm gonna eat just chicken?" he asked.

Where does this contempt come from? It lay on the journey and our lives like a great cement block. My brother with black hair, slicked to the side with stuff from a jar of white creme, a brown mole on his left cheek just above the edge of his grin, blue eyes like lucky cats' eye marbles, knew where he was going. He thought he was safe, or he just didn't care.

In the days of our journey, we were allowed to stand on the ledge between cars. That is where I went to escape the Sitting Car. I would turn my face toward our destination, my breath coming rapidly, my eyes closed, my mind reading the music of the rails that played under me, my body taking in the tremors. The wind played with my dress, pushing it up and twisting around my stomach, the wind stinging my legs until I didn't care where I was going either.

There have been times since then when I have felt that same power; the strength of my personal rage, my way of staying my own course. It was like the day I hit him with his Little League sanctioned baseball bat, chipping the bones of his elbow, for which, inevitably, fell upon me the omniscient power of Mother. I was always the criminal, my brother the victim. Mother made it self-evident, as all things were to her eye, that there would be no sibling rivalry in her family. She knew nothing of Freud, for the sustaining measure of morality was our enforced visits to confession every Saturday afternoon, when the *mea culpas* flew through the incensed drowned air and I paid a visit to the crazy God.

In the intervening years between then and somewhere close to now, I have kept the coldness with me, awaiting touches, challenging enfolding arms that are as alien to me as the thrust of an upturned finger.

THE COSMETOLOGIST

Every last Friday of the month, Evelyn Parker went to the Lakefront Mall for a haircut. It took exactly one month for her hair to take on the battered baby doll aura that had possessed her as a child. Frizzy, brittle shoots, tinted orange, sprouted from little holes in her scalp. She held them between her thumb and forefinger for inspection, wondering how it was that these twigs were really part of her. So, with the taste of baking soda and peroxide on her tongue, Evelyn left her house at exactly nine-thirty in the morning, which was a half hour before the beauty shop opened. She wanted to be first in line at the cheapest walk-in shop. She had set up this routine six months ago, ever since her son had left for college. He was her only child, and as soon as he had left her, she had started to dream about the father. They had met eighteen years ago on a night that had promised conversation, or a drink, or a touch of a hand. Evelyn had gotten all three and more at the age of thirty-eight. Now she couldn't even remember what he had looked like. He had become a fantasy, and his real name had disappeared from the list of important vestiges of her life. At night she had made her son's father the instrument of her physical pleasure. But, as soon as Joseph had gone, that too vanished. She no longer had the capacity to go crazy over anybody again, even when it was only in hidden dreams. Then the growing of her hair made her feel old, like she was slowly dissolving. She wanted the cut to be quick, no washing, no styling. Evelyn could not cope with drawn out time.

After spending three months giving each of the hairdressers at the walk-in a chance, Evelyn had picked Torcia as her favorite. Torcia was fast, did not ask personal questions, and never wasted Evelyn's time with small talk about things that really didn't matter. When Evelyn had found out that Torica was seven months pregnant under her too big yellow smock, she worried about having to make another choice. The thought of losing Torcia gave her the feeling that her body was turning to liquid. Even holding on to a chair or her kitchen counter didn't help. She came to view this impending decision as her greatest daily worry, more than aging or poverty.

This morning in July was like other Friday mornings. Florida had no season that demanded much adjustment. The sun had filled the sky every day for months now, making the air hot by eight. A drought had descended on the land, fires blazed out of control, and the rainy season had not come. When Evelyn opened the shiny glass doors and entered the mall through JC Penny, cool air embraced her and pushed back the asphalt heat that had followed her from the parking lot. The mumbled voices of the Golden Age Mall Walkers comforted her, for she saw in their brisk trots and gangly old legs a sign that blood still rushed to their hearts. She wished them well, but refused to think about the eventual need to join them. She made her way through the department store and down a path that was lined with red, green and black clothing. Evelyn neither needed nor wanted anything. She looked straight ahead of her until she reached the beauty shop just as the opening bell blasted through the mall, then the large grilled door that protected the shop rumbled open. Evelyn clutched her black plastic purse and watched the door ascend. When she looked downward and into the shop's entrance, Torcia's lucent brown face and fat belly did not greet her. An older lady with stark white hair, Prussian blue-rimmed glasses and a tremerous shaking head stood like a sentry guarding a prison. She had a short, bulky body that was wrapped in a lime green chemise. Evelyn felt a hand squeeze her heart, so she folded her arms across her chest to protect her life from flying away.

"Good morning," said a deep smoker's voice. The lady did not smile, but licked her red lips, nodded sharply and beckoned Evelyn with a wave of her plump arms.

"Welcome to Superior Cut! Come on in and let's get going. Time's a wastin'."

"I just want a fast adult cut," said Evelyn, turning to make sure that she was the only person in line. "Where's Torcia? She always cuts my hair."

"Torcia had her babies. Twins. She won't be back."

Evelyn sat in her favorite chair, positioned so that she could watch people walk by while Torcia had cut her hair. The bustling life calmed her. But now she kneaded her purse, nestling it under her forearms, wrapping the straps around her hands. Evelyn felt the chair spin until she was looking at herself in the mirror. Level with her red head, was the white head of the lady.

"My name is Hester. What kind of cut do you want?" She flipped the black plastic bib over Evelyn's head. The rush of air brought the scent of magnolia to Evelyn, and for the first time in eighteen years, the image of her mother's face flashed in her, and she gasped. The lady tied the bib around her neck, smoothed Evelyn's shoulder and said: "It will all turn out fine, dear. Just tell me what you want."

"Short, please," said Evelyn. "Just short. Make it last one month."

"You got it, kiddo," said Hester.

Evelyn felt the chair spin again. She faced the mall. A stream of children ran screaming by, followed by two young women shouting for them to be quiet. Then Evelyn felt her body move backwards until she was looking at the ceiling. "No, I don't want it washed. I don't get that," Evelyn whispered, feeling tears burn her eyes.

"Now, honey, it comes with the territory. Let me do you up good. Relax! This will make you feel real nice," said Hester.

It was a touch that Evelyn had longed for; the hands on her temples, the massaging of her scalp commanding the rest of her body to rest. She closed her eyes and thought of nothing until she felt herself rising upward and turning until she again looked at herself in the mirror. She looked different, somehow. Just different.

Hester began to cut, hands and head shaking in quick, tremulous movements, the scissors shimmering like distress signals from a far away mountain. Evelyn had seen this shaking of older people and thought of Mother. She had the same shaking the night she had banished Evelyn from her sight. Pregnant bad girl. Now she was getting a Parkinson's disease cut by jerky hands dotted with liver spots. As Hester snipped and snipped, the tremor of the hands seemed to speed up, and Evelyn's mirrored view let her imagine the glasses falling from Hester's nose and to the floor.

The smell of the beauty shop was like acid and brine, the kind that burned Evelyn's eyes when Mother poured the Toni solution on her head month after month, until her hair curled, her scalp blistered, and everyone in school laughed at her and held their noses. She had looked like a bruised plastic doll with a red clown head. Mother had said it was useless, Evelyn would never be pretty; but she did this to her every month until she was fourteen and started her period.

"I came here from Wisconsin last April. Sure is hard getting work in these small towns. Florida's hot as hell," said Hester. Her words were like bubbles popping between the clipping sound of the scissors.

Evelyn didn't want to talk, afraid that even the slightest interest would begin a commitment for months to come. She still wanted the talkless Torcia back. A sudden exhaustion crept up on her. She closed her eyes and tried to concentrate on the mall noise, the whining organ, and the static announcements about sales.

"Now I guess I have to stand on my feet cutting hair instead of playing golf. So much for dreams. It's a real bitch being alone now."

"Alone?" asked Evelyn, her eyes flying open.

"Yeah. Harold died the week after we moved here. Left me with just about nothing. So, here I am, *clip, clip, clip* like I was back in my forties."

"That's too bad," said Evelyn. In the mirror she saw a young woman, a girl, and a lady about sixty standing at the check-in desk. The lady wrote on the clipboard then stared at Hester.

"There's three of us here for cuts!" she yelled. Hester looked at the lady, grinned, nodded, then turned back to her work.

"Well, so here I am," said Hester, the words squirting out of her rounded mouth. Brown crevices of dried makeup made her look like a crone. "I don't make but minimum wage here, plus tips. Have to stand here all day just to get by. Won't get Social Security for three years. Believe it or not, my Harry was three years younger than me. Second marriage for both of us. He left me with nothing, like I said. Guess he was a liar, but man what a man!"

"I'm sorry," said Evelyn. And then she thought of a question, something she always wanted to know. "How long do you go to school to become a beautician?"

"Oh, God, seems like I went forever. Six months, I think. That was in the days before the state dogged everybody for a license. License this and license that. What do they think we're going to do, give somebody AIDS with a pair of scissors and a comb? Yep. I'm a *bona fide cosmetologist.*"

"Six months," said Evelyn. And then the words came. "Did you know that when my boy was in school, I went to a PTA meeting? A young mother named Sherry asked me if I was Joseph's grandmother. She had full, red lips and long blond hair. Very pretty. I was almost forty-six by then. My hair was long and I wore a gray dress and a black sweater with little pearls sewn along the bodice. I was embarrassed of myself, so I said yes, I was Joseph's grandmother and that his mother, my daughter, was just so busy with her job I was filling in. I lied. Then I volunteered for every committee. I waited six months, but no one called me about any more meetings."

Hester started to cut faster. The comb scraped Evelyn's right ear. Evelyn did not know why she had told that story to this cosmetologist. She longed for the end of the cut, but Hester continued to clip like a whirling helicopter.

Then Hester moved in back of Evelyn, put her hands over the sides of Evelyn's head and jerked it up. "How's that look? Just let me shave your neck a little and you're out of here. Put your head back down, honey."

Evelyn's hair had fallen to the floor and into little tufted piles, all part of her month of growing. She wanted to count each hair; maybe a thousand, she thought. The buzzing on her neck was soothing, so she closed her eyes and almost wept for joy, until the black bib was ripped from her body.

"*Voila!* That's it. Should hold you for four weeks."

Evelyn looked at her reflection, at the hair sculptured to her head like a soft, copper halo, at her black eyes now large and shining, and finally at her chin and cheeks. They had lost the sag that had made her look abandoned. She was the image of the woman she needed to be, her lips now curled up in a smile. "Thanks," she said, and opened her purse, searching for the twenty dollar bill she kept hidden in the little zippered pocket for an emergency.

Hester had moved to the reception desk and was punching at the register with her stubby index finger. "Nine ninety-five," she said.

Evelyn handed her the twenty dollar bill and turned away, quickly walking into the cool air of the mall. The soft tinkling of a piano was cheering, then the blast of trumpets that followed seemed to call her. *Come! Come now! We're a live band!* Evelyn Parker turned toward the music and not toward home.

"Wait! Wait up!" boomed a voice. Evelyn turned slowly and

faced Hester's hand quivering in her face, red nails flashing. "Here, take my calling card for when you come back next month." The card was bright pink like Pepto-Bismal. Neon blue stars surrounded bold gold script that read: *Hester Jane Billing. Cosmetologist by walk-in, Spiritual Counseling by appointment only.*

About the Author

L.M. Young was born and raised in Southwestern Louisiana. Her short fiction has appeared in the Bishop's House Review. She is a past contributor to the Bread Loaf Writer's Conference. She now lives in the Smoky Mountains of North Carolina.